Truths #101

Timeless secrets for making life work

'Lola Ogunjimi

#101 Truths

Timeless secrets for making life work

'Lola Ogunjimi

Copyright © 2018 by Lola Ogunjimi. All rights reserved.

ISBN: 978-1-64440-353-2

Email: lolaogunjimipublishing@gmail.com

Cover design & page layout by www.wearereach.org

No part of this book may be reprinted or utilised in any form or by any means, electronic or mechanical, including, but not limited to, photocopying or recording, or by any information storage or retrieval system, without permission in writing from the publisher.

Truths #101

Timeless secrets for
making life work

Words spoken at the right time are like gold apples
in a silver setting.

Proverbs 25:11 (CEB)

To Toni, Tolu and Temi

I am blessed to have three beautiful daughters.

You are, individually, such an inspiration.

ACKNOWLEDGEMENTS

My mum, Yetunde Fayoyin, and a couple of my friends, Louise Davies and Noida Darien-Campbell, individually kept asking when I was going to write again after my first devotional, 'I'm A Mum Get Me Outta Here'. It's been a long time coming but thanks for your constant asking, it spurred me to get this done.

Thank you, Lou, for taking the time to read through my initial draft and giving such valuable feedback and advice.

To my husband, Yinka, and our daughters, Toni, Tolu and Temi, for all the support and encouragement. Special thanks to Tolu for the art work.

Most of all, to God, my ever-present Father; this is for your glory.

INTRODUCTION

As I go through each day, I am amazed at how present God is and his interest in the details of our lives. He speaks through the daily circumstances we go through, wanting to help us make a success of life.

I have written #101 Truths as an easy read; each page conveying a thought which I trust you can readily understand and relate to. My desire is that you will be encouraged and strengthened by the truths, scriptures and promises on each page. I chose a hundred and one because the number denotes an introductory, a starting point. Each day's devotional is just a starting point of all God has to say. Taking time, through the day, to think on the day's writing will lead to fuller insight and application.

I pray that what you read each day will be for you, the right word at the right time, causing you to increase in the knowledge of the truth of God's love for you and his presence with you always.

Lola

Each devotional is just a starting point of what God has to say. Taking time through your day to carefully meditate on what is read will lead to fuller insight and application. To assist mindful reflection the verses for each day is set within a patterned border which can be coloured in.

#makingupthedifference

It is Father's Day as I write this and as you do, I thought about my dad and something that happened a long time ago. I must have been about thirteen, it was my parents' wedding anniversary and I really wanted to get them a present.

I got them four wine glasses, asked the shop keeper to put them in a box and very proudly took them home. When Dad got back, I couldn't wait for him to open the present. He smiled and said, "Thank you." A second later he asked, "But why are there two missing?" I was kind of hoping he wouldn't notice the two empty spaces! "That was all I could afford," I said, rather sadly. Dad took me back to the shop, we got a couple more glasses and completed the set.

To me, that's just a picture of what our Heavenly Father has done. We all have sinned and come up short, but Jesus went to the cross and paid the full price we could never afford so we can enjoy complete, abundant lives.

Thank you, dear Father, for making up the difference so that I can have a full relationship with you.

#bigbrother

Imagine the lovely feeling, walking through the high school gate as a new pupil, knowing your big brother is head boy! There is a confidence, "Nobody can touch me!"

Some days, it seems like I'm being taunted but I hold my nerve; My big brother, Jesus Christ, is head over all!

There is no place for fear, knowing he is near.

Thank you, Father, for your continuous presence with me.

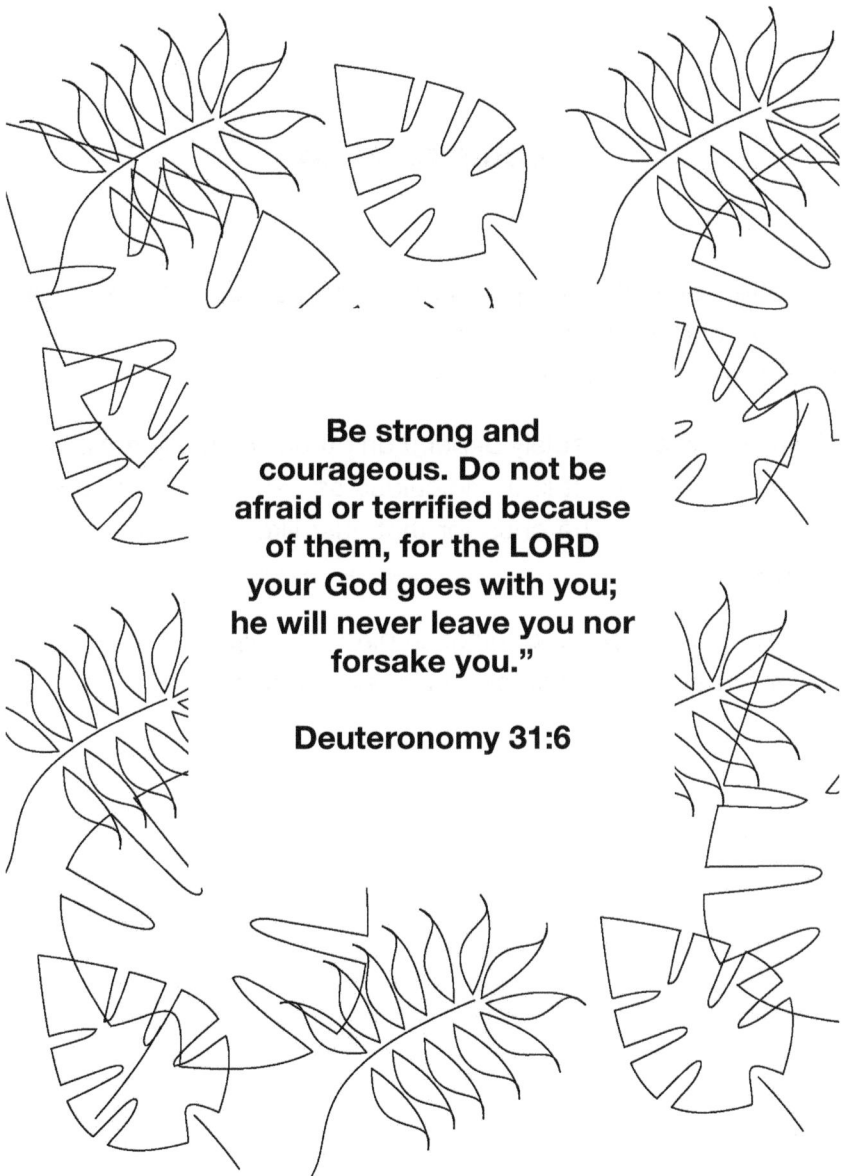

Be strong and courageous. Do not be afraid or terrified because of them, for the LORD your God goes with you; he will never leave you nor forsake you."

Deuteronomy 31:6

#bodybuilding

We often expect other people to build us up; our pastor, our spouse, our employer. We are looking at these people to make us better in one way or the other.

However, when we solely depend on others we really are asking too much of them. It is as ridiculous as expecting someone to exercise for you! The onus for that, just like our spiritual build, is ours.

God will put people and things in place to help us, but we must never forget, building ourselves is our responsibility.

**Thank you, Lord, for showing me how
I can be strong in you.**

But ye, beloved, building up yourselves on your most holy faith, praying in the Holy Ghost

Jude 1:20 (KJV)

#tomorrowsworld

My daughter was facing key exams but, in my mind, wasn't adequately preparing for them so I started nagging her about what she was doing.

Needless to say, it didn't go down well and God intervened by telling me to stop describing to her what I could see but rather speak beyond it. In other words, rather than describe the valley of dry bones, prophesy and speak into existence what I wanted to see.

What does your tomorrow's world look like?

Start declaring it today!

Thank you, Lord, for the power today to change my tomorrow.

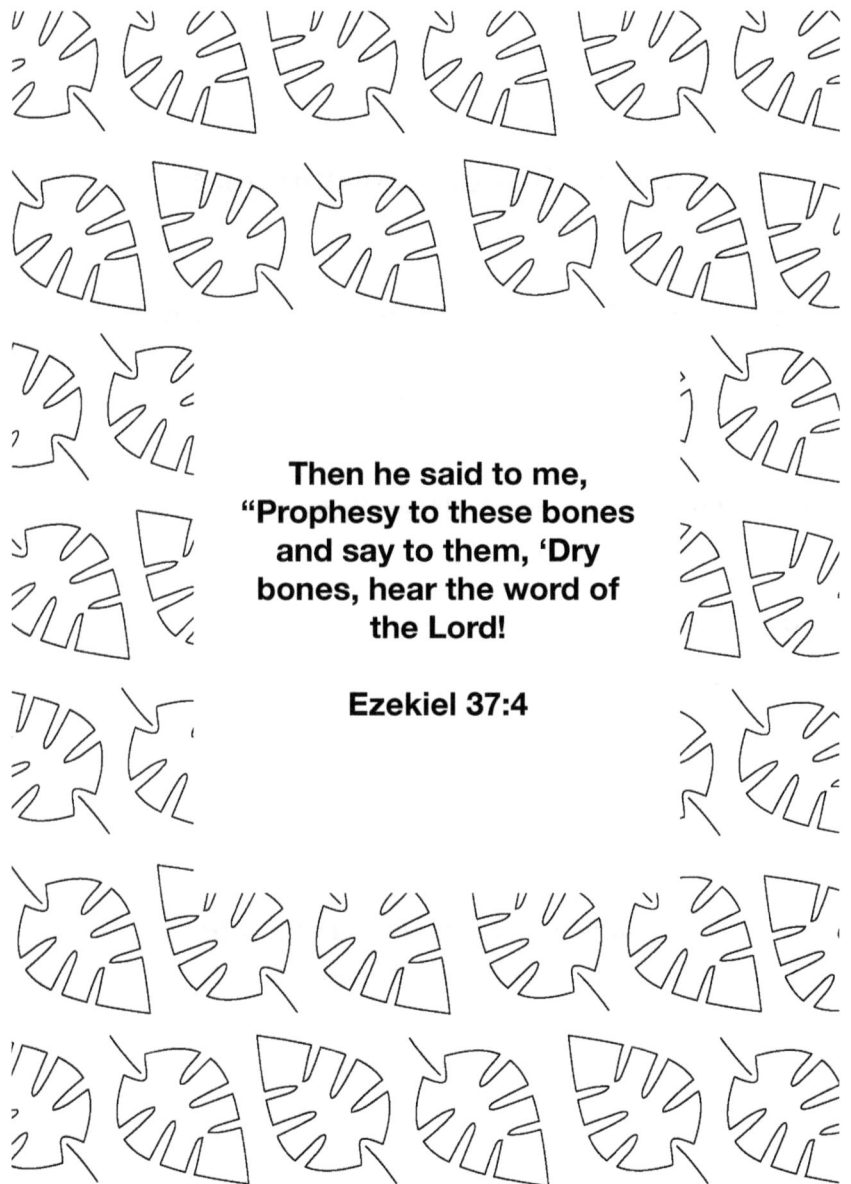

Then he said to me, "Prophesy to these bones and say to them, 'Dry bones, hear the word of the Lord!

Ezekiel 37:4

#lifeinstructionsfordummies

When trying to put together a flat pack, we can sometimes get by without the instructions. However, when it comes to putting together the life that pleases God, we really can't afford to ignore the instructions he has given to us in the Bible.

Knowing humans though, God has made it simple by summing up his instructions in two points:

1) Love God

2) Love people

The One who made us knows far best how we should live and we will do well to heed his instructions.

Thank you, Lord, for making your instructions clear to me.

Jesus answered, "The most important is, 'Hear, O Israel: The Lord our God, the Lord is one. And you shall love the Lord your God with all your heart and with all your soul and with all your mind and with all your strength.' The second is this: 'You shall love your neighbour as yourself.' There is no other commandment greater than these."

Mark 12:29-31

#givememyanswer

It's not just children who do it —shopping around for an answer —adults do too! For the child it may be going from one parent to the other, hoping for a more suitable response, but as adults we have more sources for our answer.

Some consult the internet, others the television and some, friends. There is only one when it comes to the question of our life though. The source is the Word of God, the Bible, and the answer is Jesus Christ.

We can shop around all we like but Jesus is the only way by which we can be saved, and the Bible is the only guide as to how we ought to live.

Thank you, Jesus, for being my saviour.

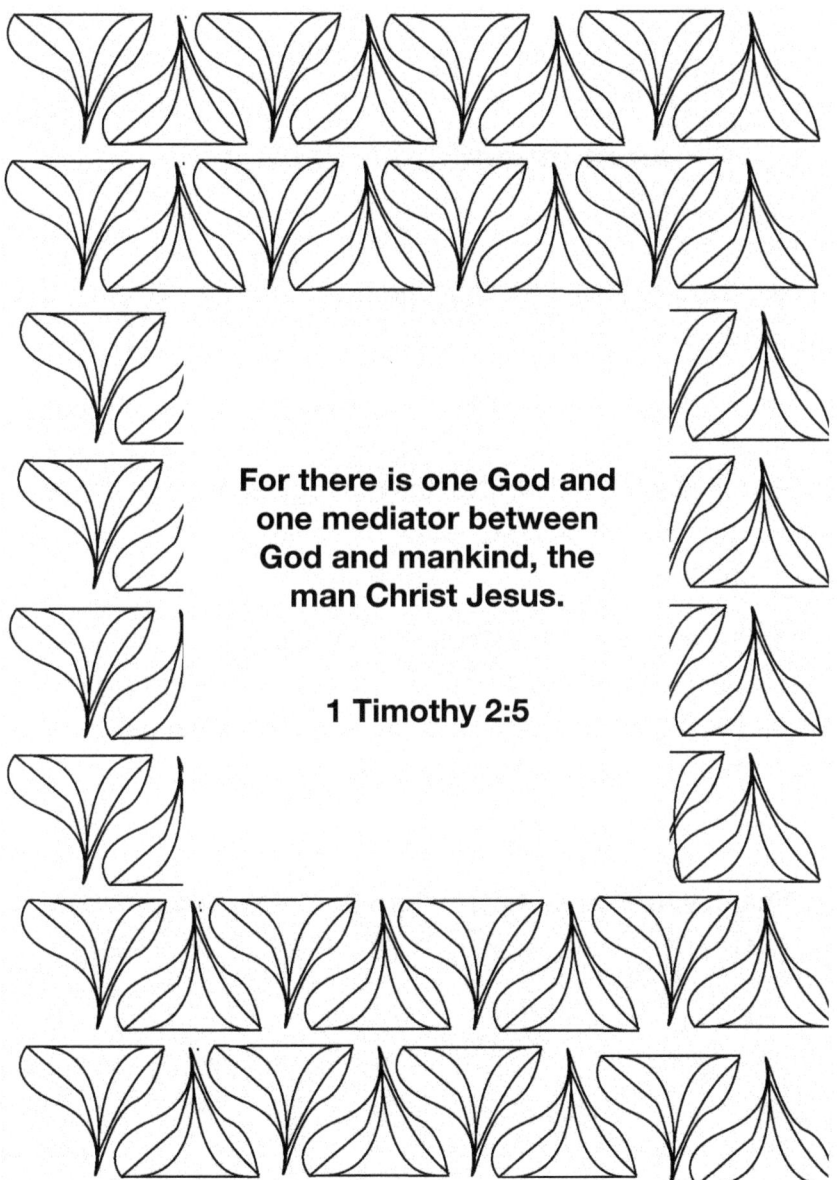

For there is one God and one mediator between God and mankind, the man Christ Jesus.

1 Timothy 2:5

#idontneedthatkindofmoney

Money is money, isn't it? Or is there any kind of money we are better off without?

Sitting on the train, I overheard a gentleman talking to his colleague about childcare. I didn't really hear the question he was asked but he responded, "No, the grandparents were not registered, and I wasn't going to fiddle the system. I don't need that kind of money."

I secretly commended the man for his wisdom. I don't know if he'd read the Bible or not, but he was certainly operating by the word of wisdom in Proverbs that implies, money gained by devious means is the kind of money we do not need.

Thank you, Father, for wisdom that helps me prosper.

Dishonest money dwindles away, but whoever gathers money little by little makes it grow.

Proverbs 13:11

#safetygatesandplaypens

My niece turned one recently and her mum told me she was getting into everything, so they had constructed a large playpen for her. It made her parents happier to know she could play safely within the frame.

The Bible, in effect, makes us understand God has us within a frame. Living within the safety of his laws our lives are protected.

Not understanding the love and care of her parents, I'm sure my niece didn't always appreciate the boundary of her playpen or the fact there were safety gates around the house. In the same way, we may not always understand the why of God's commands, but we can trust it all stems from his unfailing love for us.

Thank Lord for the boundary you have set around my life.

Moreover by them is thy servant warned: and in keeping of them there is great reward.

Psalm 19:11 (KJV)

#crueltobekind

I was in a taxi not long ago and the 1979 single by Nick Lowe, *Cruel to be kind*, came on the radio. The lyrics of the chorus are as follows:

You've gotta be cruel to be kind, in the right measure

Cruel to be kind, it's a very good sign

Cruel to be kind, means that I love you baby

(You've gotta be cruel)

You gotta be cruel to be kind

As I listened, I could not help but think about the times I heard a parent say, "I am correcting you because I love you." Of course, as a child, I never believed that. As a parent though, I know just how true it is for I love my girls and want the best for them. More than that, I know it is true because God's word says so. He says, *"For the LORD corrects those he loves, just as a father corrects a child in whom he delights*[1]*."*

If you sense God's correction today, remember, he loves you!

Thank you, Father, for your corrections.

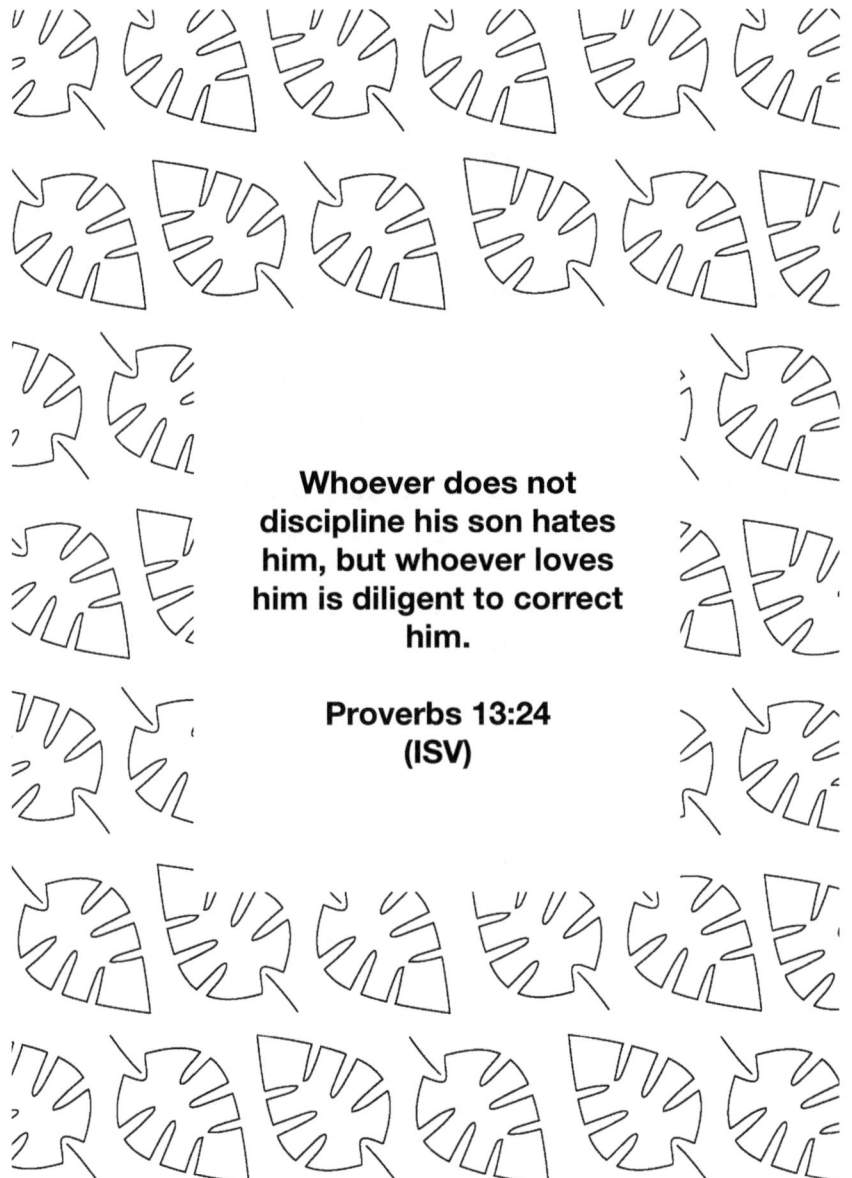

Whoever does not discipline his son hates him, but whoever loves him is diligent to correct him.

Proverbs 13:24 (ISV)

#fullypresent

The response of "Mmh," was not at all what I was expecting. I'd asked a question and that was not the correct reply! We've all had those experiences when the person who is around and supposedly listening to us, isn't giving us full attention.

Thankfully, our Father God is ever fully present. The Bible recounts he is a very present help in our time of trouble.

Whatever you are going through today, you can be confident God is fully present with you and attentively listening to all you say.

**Thank you, Father, for your full presence
with me always.**

God is our refuge and strength, a very present help in trouble.

Psalm 46:1 (KJV)

#idontcarewhattheweathermansays

We love to talk about the weather, here in the UK. It can be very variable and so a great conversation opener. To counter complaints about being hindered by the weather, it is often said, "There is no such thing as bad weather, only inappropriate clothing."

Journeying through life sometimes can seem like the changing UK weather. One minute the sun is shining and the next minute the storms appear!

The only covering that can help us face whatever the weather of life may throw our way is Jesus Christ. If we don't know Him, personally, as Lord and Saviour then we just aren't appropriately dressed for life.

Let me encourage you, if you don't know Jesus as Saviour, now is as good a time as any to make that decision. Turn to the back of the book to and find out more about inviting Jesus Christ into your life.

Thank you, Jesus, for dying to give me your life.

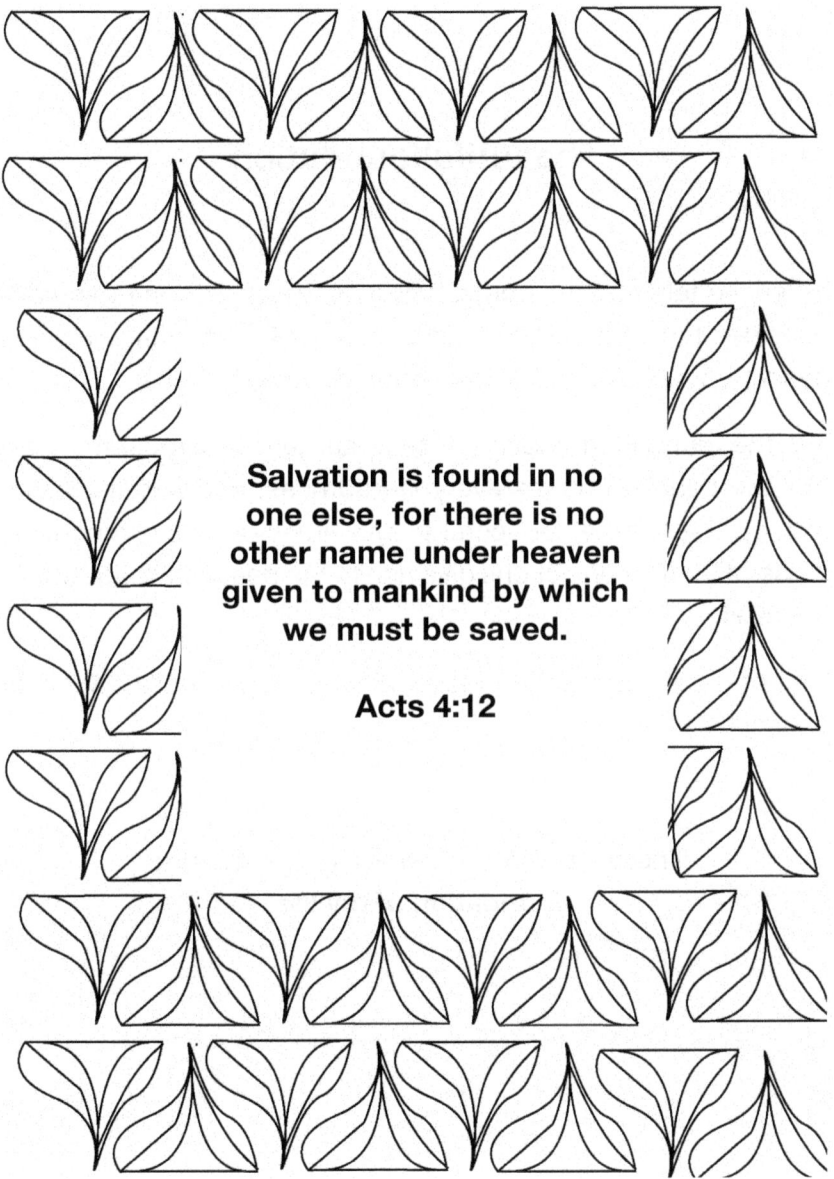

Salvation is found in no one else, for there is no other name under heaven given to mankind by which we must be saved.

Acts 4:12

#beautifulfoundation

When we talk about a house being beautiful we don't generally consider the foundation. I have heard of a foundation being described as solid or firm but never as being beautiful.

It is the foundation, though unseen and unglamorous, that carries the beautiful house everyone admires, and it is the same with our lives. Whether secret prayer times or acts of kindness, those often unseen actions give rise to the beautiful things about our lives.

Do not underestimate foundational work, it produces a thing of beauty.

Thank you, Jesus, that you are the firm foundation of my life.

Everyone who comes to me and hears my words and does them, I will show you what he is like: he is like a man building a house, who dug deep and laid the foundation on the rock.

Luke 6:47 - 48
(ESV)

#makethemgiants

Our words can either build others up or pull them down and we have a choice as to which we do. Sometimes, in the heat of an argument or in response to a mean remark, we may be tempted to tear people down. However, the admonishment is to only say what will lift them up.

So, regardless of what others may say or do today, make it your aim to only respond with a kind word.

Thank you, Father, for teaching and helping me to speak kindly.

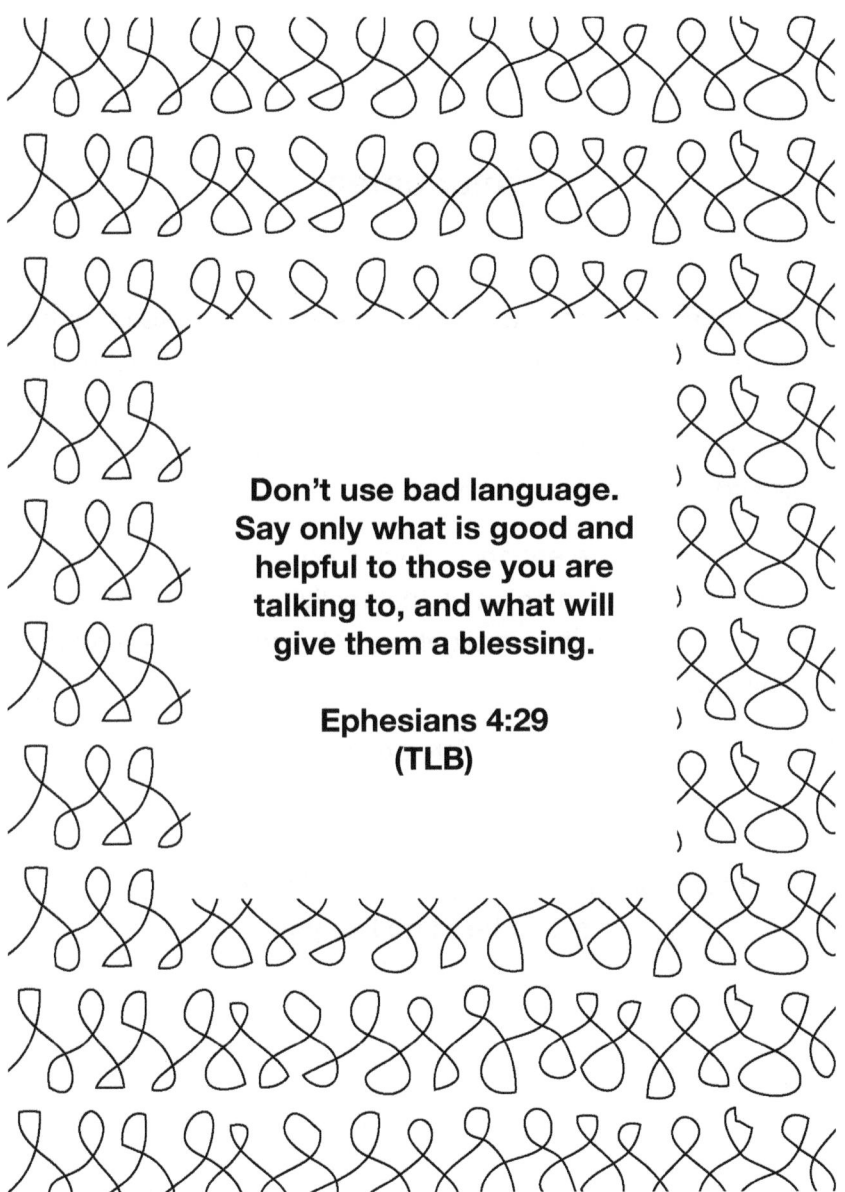

Don't use bad language. Say only what is good and helpful to those you are talking to, and what will give them a blessing.

Ephesians 4:29
(TLB)

#marinated

My daughter and I have a thing against eating chicken that has not been well marinated. Yes, you can season the chicken just before you cook it, but that seasoning is not as effective as when the seasoning is left a while to really get into the meat before it is cooked. It really does taste different.

The Bible says, *"The entrance of your word gives light"*. It is the word that we allow to get in us that really makes a difference in our lives. How does the word get in us? It is when we spend time mediating on it.

Today, set time aside to mediate on the word of God.

Lord, thank you that your word in me changes me to be more like you.

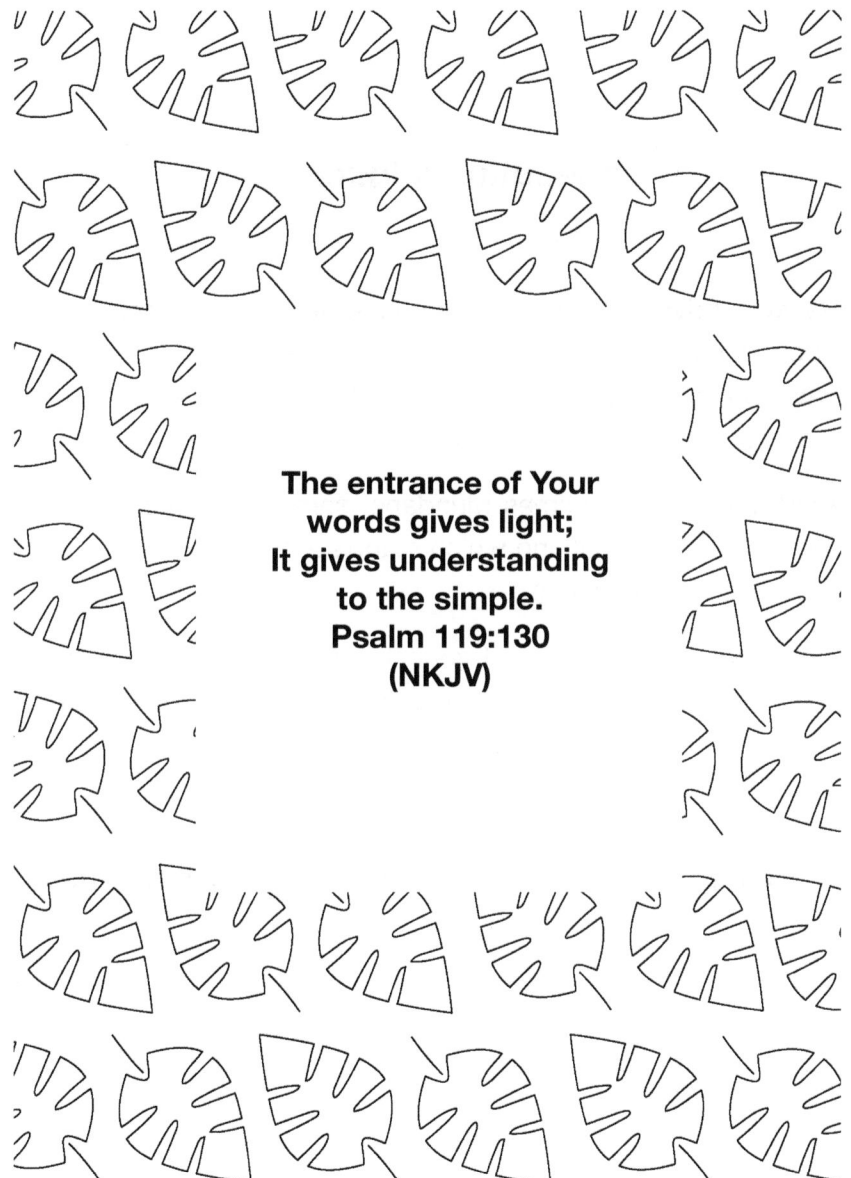

The entrance of Your words gives light; It gives understanding to the simple.
Psalm 119:130
(NKJV)

#beautifuluniqueness

We were driving down a country lane. It was row upon row of green bushes and trees and then we came across a purple flowering bush. Its uniqueness to all that surrounded it only intensified its rich colour and beauty.

Amid our day, sometimes mundane; same old same old, God always places something which stands a beautiful testimony of his love and faithfulness.

I pray that as you go about your day, God will open your eyes to his greatness and all the unique things he has placed around you.

Thank you so much, Lord, for the beauty all around me.

LORD, the earth is filled with your faithful love

Psalm 119:64 (CSB)

#silentwitness

I love detective and legal TV shows. It is interesting to watch the effort expended to get a witness one to the stand when they can help a case.

God has expended the greatest of powers, the Holy Spirit, to enable us to testify to his splendour and majesty. No witness is called who has nothing to say. So, regardless of what our testimony is, God wants us to use it.

Today, don't be a silent witness.

Thank you, Lord, for trusting me to be a witness for you.

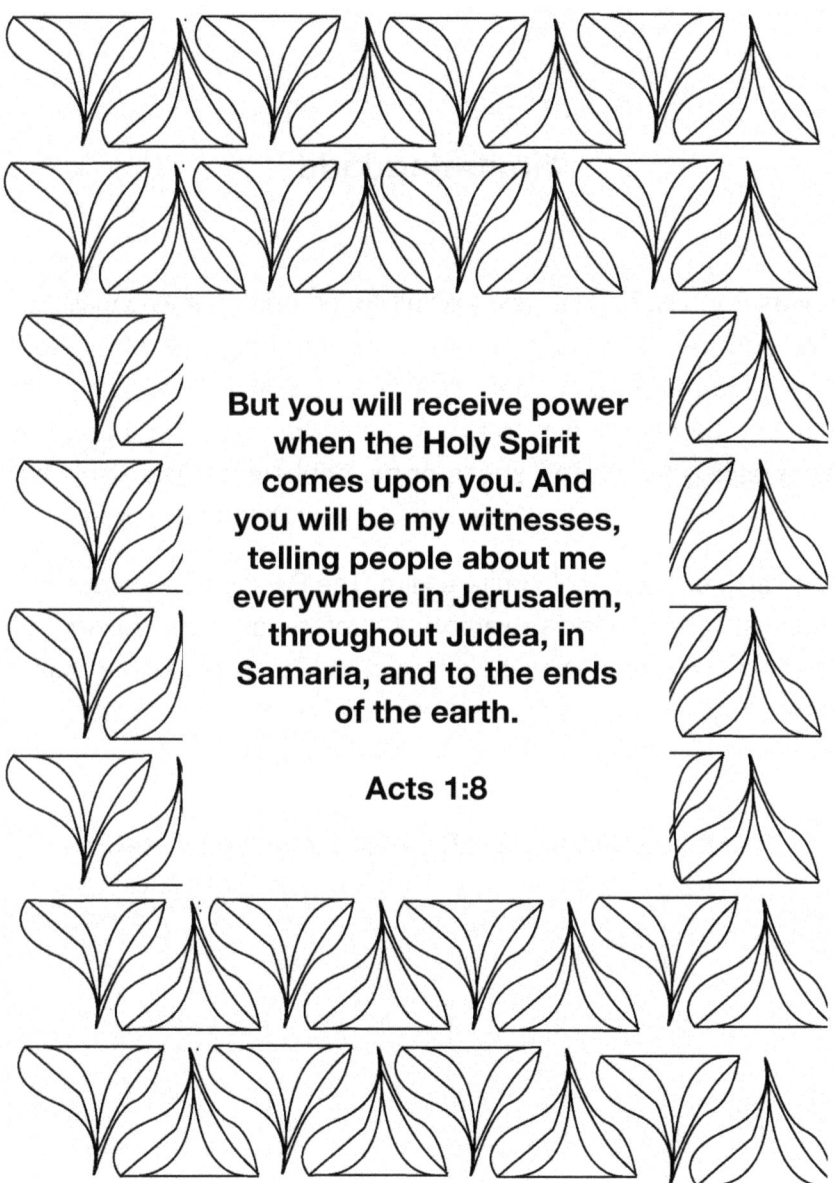

But you will receive power when the Holy Spirit comes upon you. And you will be my witnesses, telling people about me everywhere in Jerusalem, throughout Judea, in Samaria, and to the ends of the earth.

Acts 1:8

#imitatingdaddy

It was Sunday, my nephew was all suited up, but it was well past church time. Curious, I asked, "Why don't you get changed?" "Oh," his mum responded, "He likes dressing like daddy and you can hardly get him to take his suit off." Whether it is a little girl wearing her mum's shoes or my nephew not taking his suit off, it is well known that children love imitating their parents.

God also expects us to imitate Him. The Bible (in Ephesians 5:1-2) says, *"Follow God's example, therefore, as dearly loved children and walk in the way of love, just as Christ loved us and gave himself up for us as a fragrant offering and sacrifice to God."*

Thank you, Father, for the example you have set me.

**I have given you an
example to follow.
Do as I have done to you.**

**John 13:15
(NLT)**

#keepsafe

After my oldest daughter was born, I admit to doing what most first-time parents have often done; check she was still breathing and okay as she slept. As she grew up, I did that less but in other ways worried about her safety and that of her younger sisters, when they came along.

I couldn't always be with them to check they were okay and so had to trust them to the only person I knew could watch over them constantly.

Whether your child is at the baby stage or even have babies of their own, you are always the parent. Rather than fret over them you, you can trust the God who will keep them safe always.

Thank you, Father, for your watchful eyes over my loved ones.

Our children will live in safety, and under your protection their descendants will be secure.

Psalm 102:28 (GNT)

#ayeayecaptain

Psalm 1 verse 6 in the Message Bible says, *"God charts the road you take."* I picture a board with lots of different coloured pins; the charting of my life and yours. It is a detailed record of the path of each of our lives so far and an exact pinpoint of where we are just now.

More than that, God has charted every detail of our lives for the future and it is good.

All we need to do is agree with the captain of our lives and say, "Aye aye," to his pathway.

Thank you, Lord, for being the captain of my life.

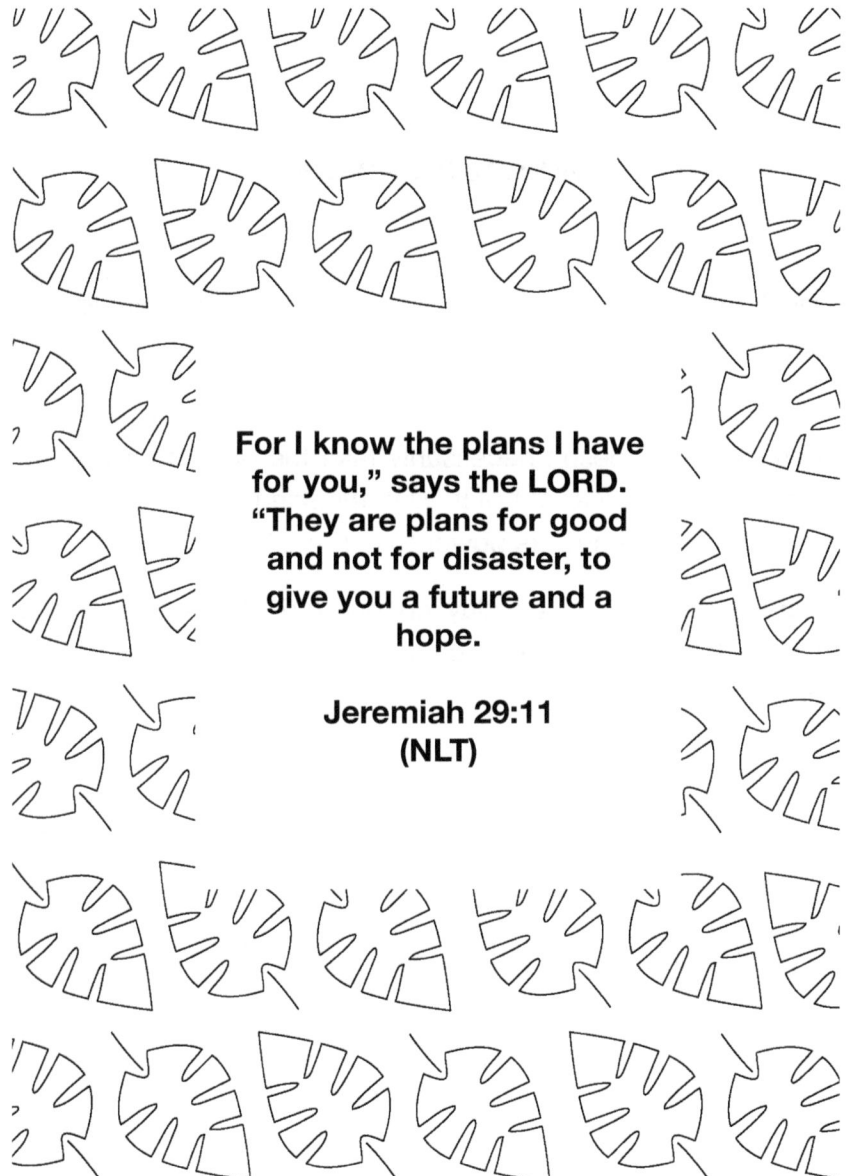

For I know the plans I have for you," says the LORD. "They are plans for good and not for disaster, to give you a future and a hope.

**Jeremiah 29:11
(NLT)**

#dadtotherescue

"Dad!" it was loud and shrill. It was simple; she was afraid and wanted the bee removed.

I often cry out to our heavenly Father about issues too. Sometimes I find he doesn't necessarily take the problem away but instead takes the fear out of it. With the sting gone, I can shrug at the problem. I know its power to hurt me has been removed.

Whatever you are facing today, cry out to God then trust him to answer; dealing with the problem in whichever way he deems best.

Thank you, Father, for attending to my cry.

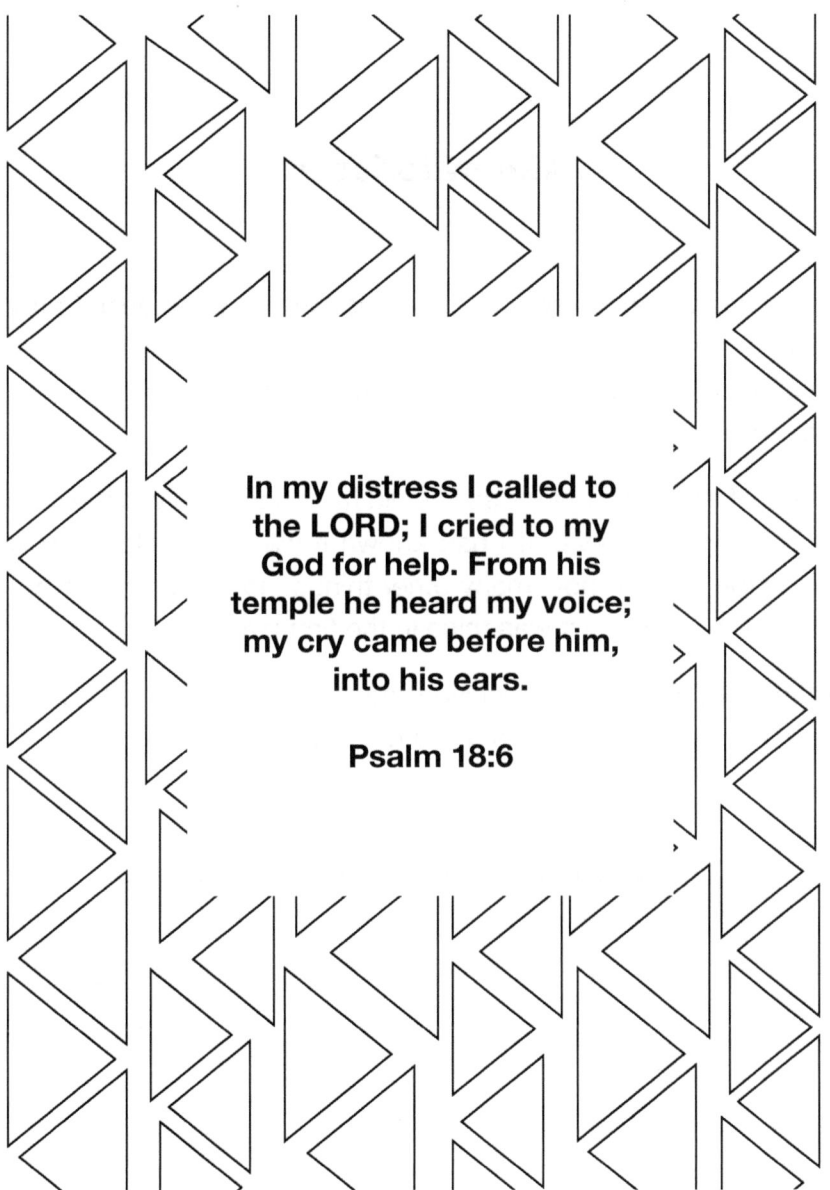

In my distress I called to the LORD; I cried to my God for help. From his temple he heard my voice; my cry came before him, into his ears.

Psalm 18:6

#knowitorloseit

I once didn't recognise an item of clothing as mine despite my daughter trying hard to convince me. "I'll happily have it," she said finally, "but I do know it is yours." Later, I realised it really was mine, but I had 'lost it'.

It was of no consequence as I would have happily given the item of clothing away even if I had known it was mine. However, it made me wonder how many other things I lose out on just because I didn't know it was mine in the first place.

Thankfully, we have all received the Holy Spirit who tells us all that is ours in Christ Jesus. Let's not argue otherwise!

Thank you, Lord, for the gift of the Holy Spirit.

We have not received this world's spirit; instead, we have received the Spirit sent by God, so that we may know all that God has given us.

1 Corinthians

#hungryforsomething

Sometimes we know exactly what we want to eat. Other times, we know we want something but aren't sure what. We have one snack after the other, but none really hits the mark.

God satisfies the longings we know and can articulate, the ones we know but can't quite find the words for and those we don't even know about.

Yes, God knows and wants to satisfy the deep longings in our spirit.

Thank you, Father, for satisfying all my needs.

For he satisfies the longing soul, and the hungry soul he fills with good things.

Psalm 107:9 (ESV)

#righttoolforthejob

I walked into the room, about to have a procedure done, and noticed the various sized instruments laid out. I might have panicked but I've had the same dentist for several years now and trusted him to use the right instrument to get the job done.

The truth is that sometimes, despite my knowledge of the Father's good character and intentions, I'm rather wary of the instruments he uses.

However, whether it is someone who rubs us up the wrong way to teach tolerance or some seemingly delayed answer to teach patience, we need not fear. God's word expressly states he wisely knows to use just the right tool to get the job done.

Father, thank you that your thoughts towards me are always good.

The wheels of a threshing cart may be rolled over it, but one does not use horses to grind grain. All this also comes from the Lord Almighty, whose plan is wonderful, whose wisdom is magnificent.

Isaiah 28:28b-29

#behappy

It had the picture of a radio, animated with a smiley face and the wording on the billboard was, 'Set your mood to good.' I liked it a lot because it reminded me my mood was my choice and not necessarily a consequence of my current situation.

Our circumstances will change, sometimes very favourably and other times not so much, however, our mood doesn't have to fluctuate like a yoyo. Each one of us can choose to be joyful, always. It is a decision that will alter our demeanour.

Thank you Lord I can rejoice in you always.

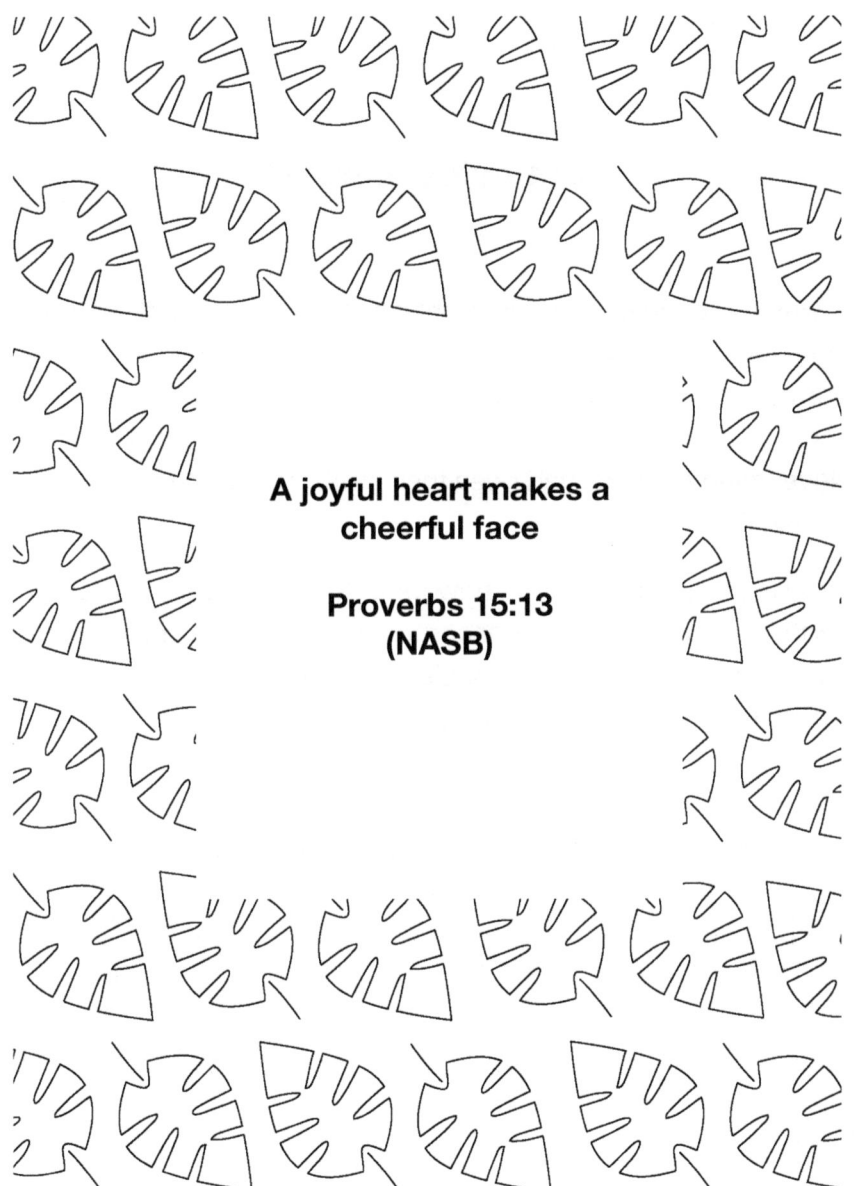

A joyful heart makes a cheerful face

**Proverbs 15:13
(NASB)**

#butmyteachersaid

It was great when they were pre-school age and took as gospel everything I said. However, one by one, as my girls started primary school, they would often say to me, "... but my teacher said ...," and regardless of what I said, the teacher was right. Never mind the fact I had been their mother longer than they had known the teacher!

Our Heavenly father, who knew us before the foundation of the earth, has spoken good concerning us. It doesn't matter what our circumstances or anyone else says, we need to hold God's word as the highest authority for our lives.

Thank you, Father, for your dependable word.

Your way is perfect, Lord, and your word is correct.

Psalm 18:30 (CEV)

#periscope

When submerged in situations or behind obstacles it is often hard to see beyond the difficulty of what we face and that is when our periscope, called faith, comes in handy.

Our faith allows us to see beyond the immediate and get a full view of the things that are otherwise out of sight; all that is ours in Jesus.

Being confident of what is just out of sight should change how we live today and every other day.

Thank you, Father, that in you I am confident of so much more.

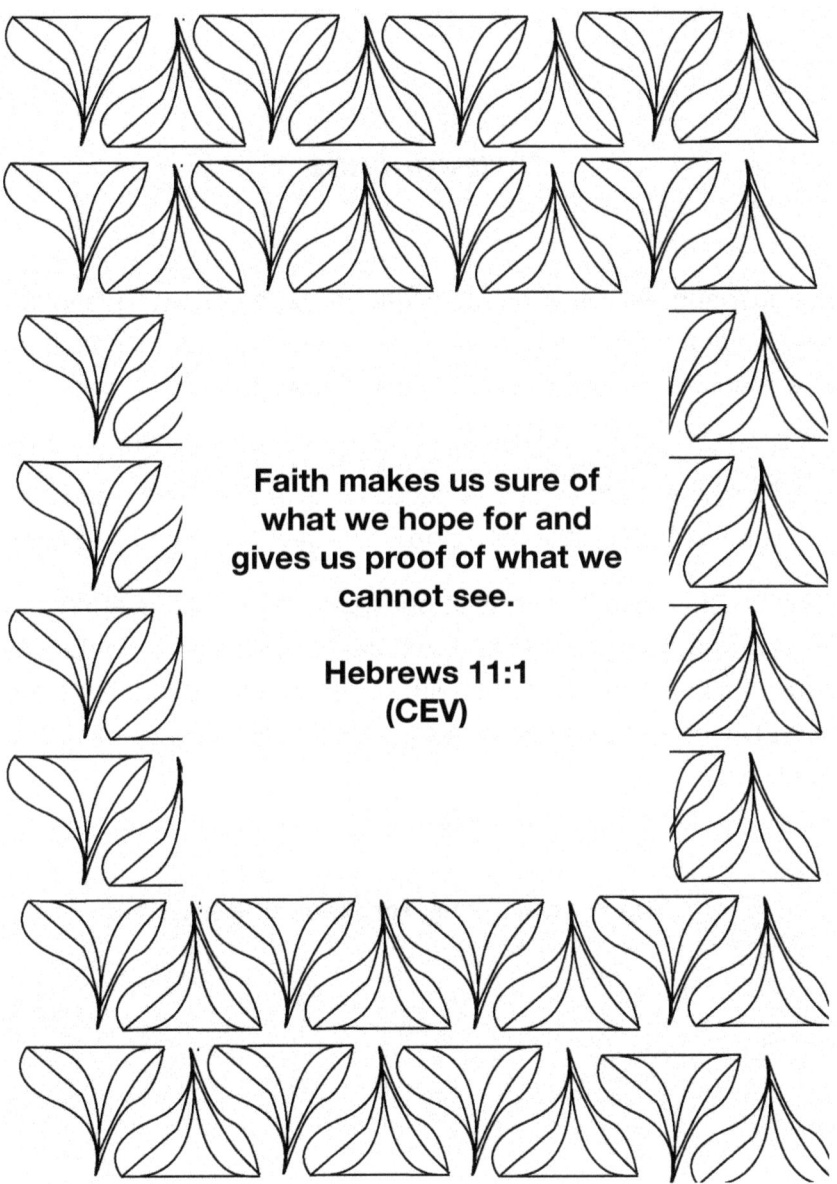

Faith makes us sure of what we hope for and gives us proof of what we cannot see.

Hebrews 11:1 (CEV)

#cleanhands

My husband, recounting his childhood experiences, mentioned his primary school assembly often included a hand inspection. The teachers came around checking that pupils had cut their nails and that their hands were clean.

Our heavenly Father also expects us to have clean hands. In *1 Timothy 2:8*, the Bible talks about us lifting holy hands, to God.

Clean hands reflect what is in our heart; right actions springing from a right heart. If, in truth, we have received the righteousness which is from God, by faith in Jesus, then by faith we are already clean and can boldly lift our hearts and hands and bless the Lord.

Thank you, Jesus, for cleansing me.

Nevertheless, the righteous will hold to their ways, and those with clean hands will grow stronger.

Job 17:9

#fasttrainslow

I was sat on what was meant to be a fast train into London. Instead, we were travelling at snail speed. A signal failure meant we could not go as fast as expected. I could walk quicker, I thought to myself, rather irritated by the slow pace.

Often, I want things done quickly. I am learning though that God is never in the hurry I am in. I want things changed in an instant. He is more interested in taking his time to change me.

Regardless of how quick or slow your journey is today, be sure to know God's timing is best.

Thank you, Lord, for teaching me to be patient.

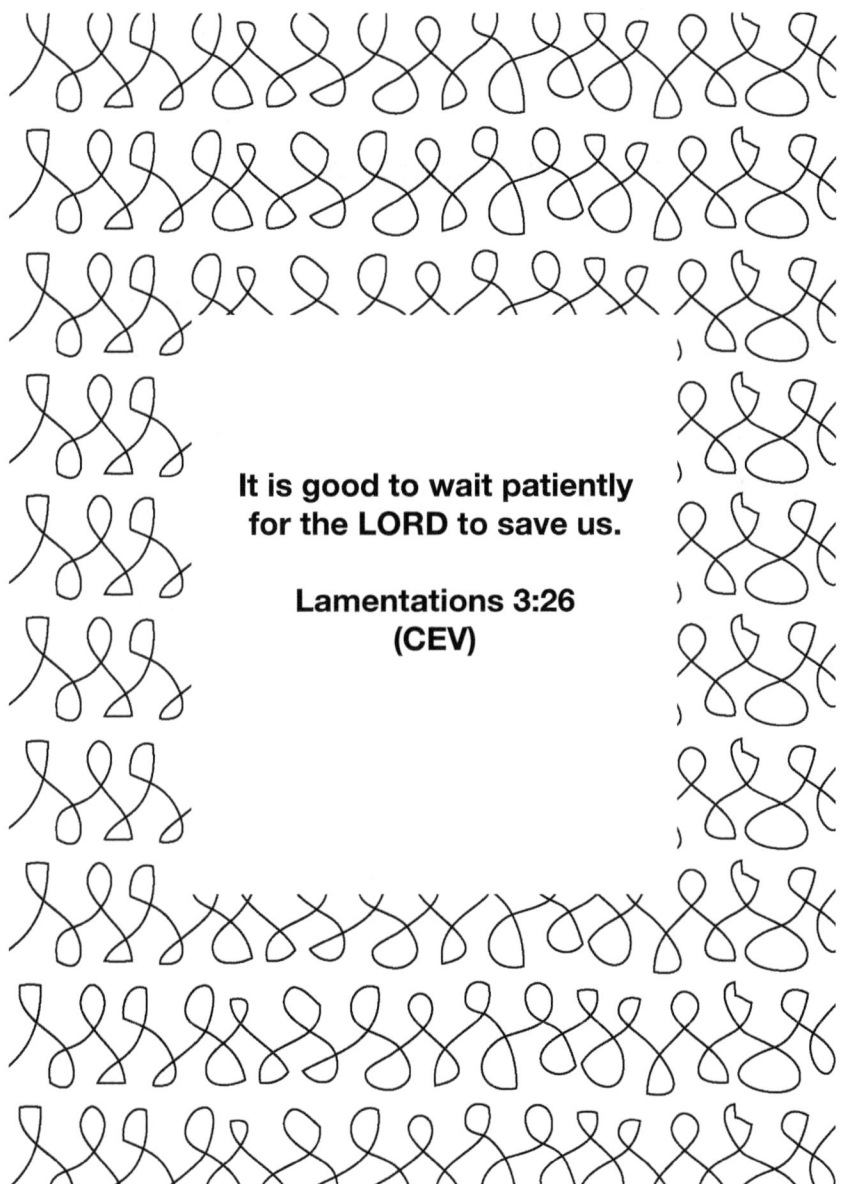

It is good to wait patiently for the LORD to save us.

Lamentations 3:26 (CEV)

#rightanswer

"Sorry," was not the response my daughter was expecting. She'd reported that her younger sister had just poured orange juice on her head. The response she got made her wonder if her dad had really heard her.

Sometimes, I wonder the same about God. Did he hear my prayer or is it that he just doesn't care to give the expected answer?

Reminding myself of God's constant faithfulness helps me through those times. Even when it doesn't appear so, he does care, and his response is always right.

Thank you, Father, for your care and right responses always.

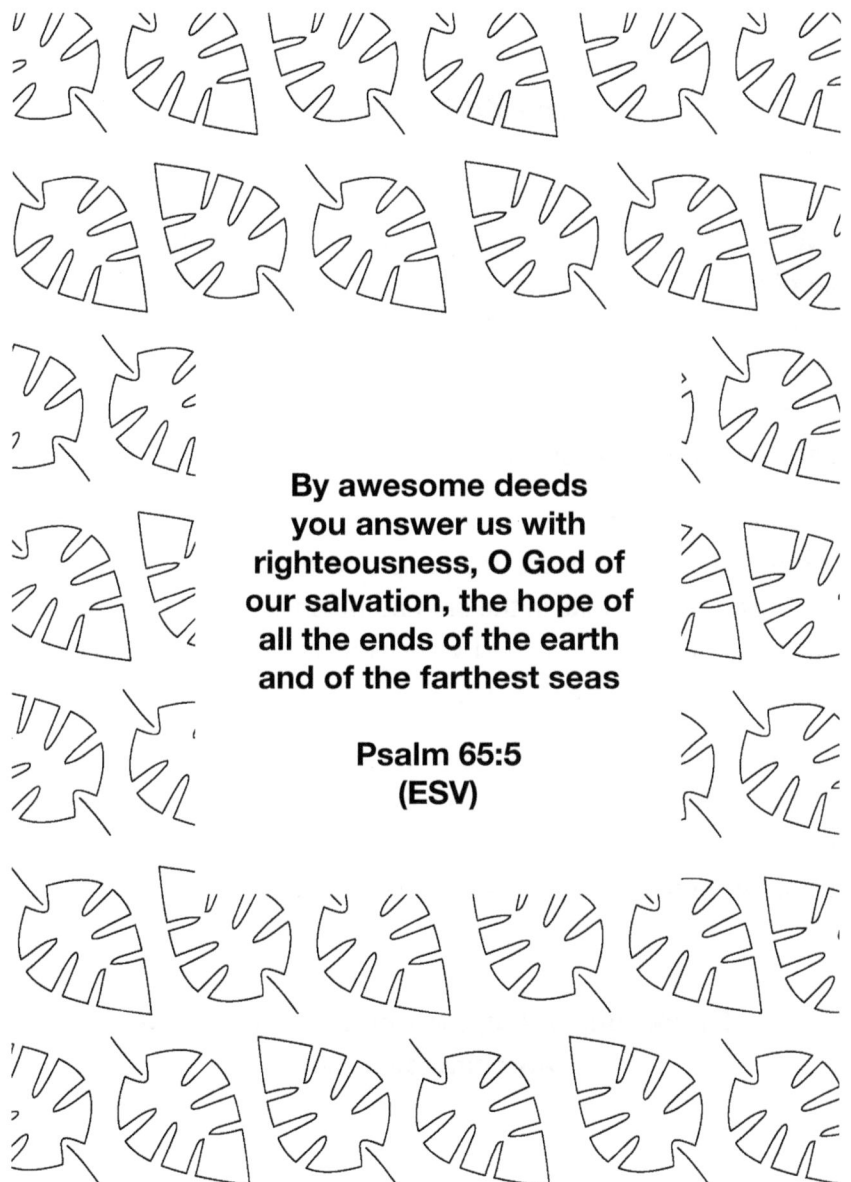

By awesome deeds you answer us with righteousness, O God of our salvation, the hope of all the ends of the earth and of the farthest seas

Psalm 65:5 (ESV)

#eyesonthechild

A very long time ago when my now twenty-something year old daughter was a toddler, we were on a long car journey when we broke down and had to pull up on the side of the road. It was a very hot summer day, so we opened the passenger side doors for more air and got in conversation whilst we waited for the roadside recovery assistance.

Suddenly we were interrupted by the loud beeping of a car horn. Something about it made me jump and think, "Oh no, where is she?" The three adults in the car had taken our eyes off the baby and my inquisitive child had wandered to the side of the road. Thankfully, no harm was done.

Our Heavenly Father never gets so engrossed with anything that he loses sight of us, not even for a second. Wherever you are and whatever you are doing today, you can be sure God's ever watchful eyes are on you to keep you safe.

Thank you, Father, for your loving eyes ever watching over me.

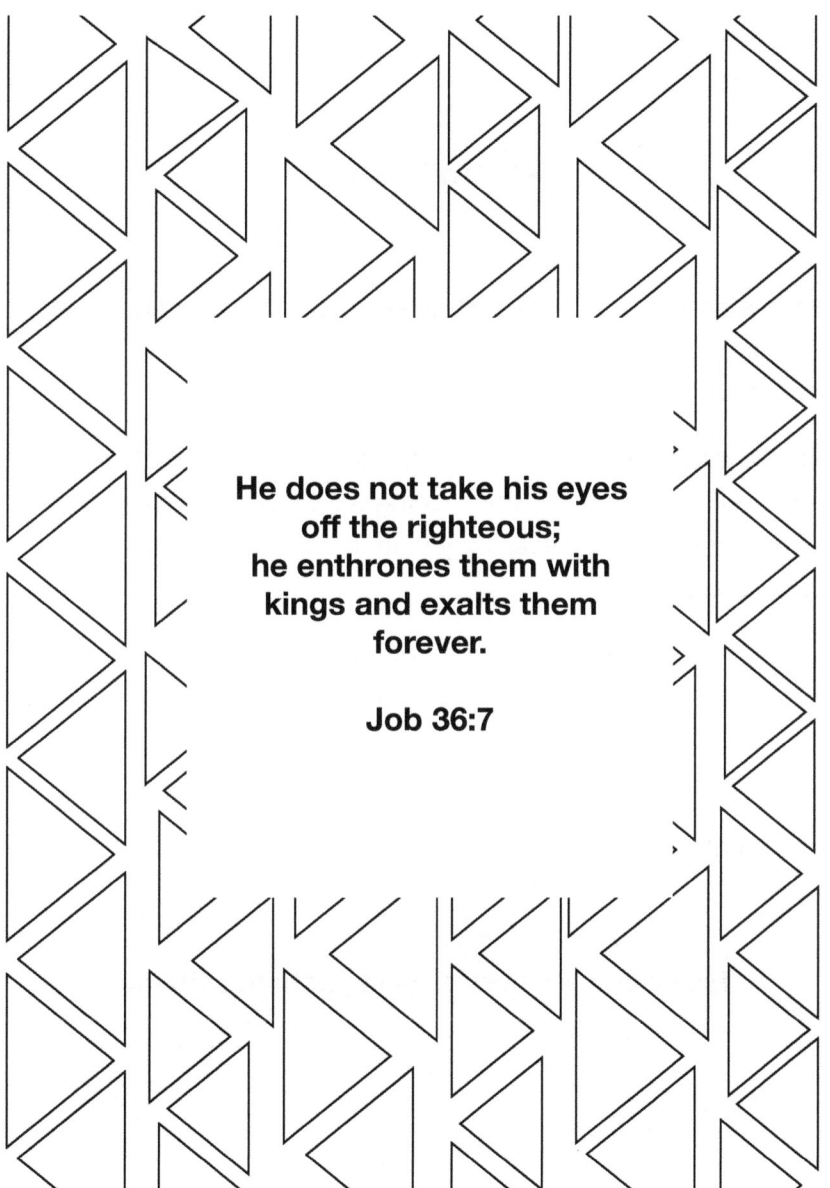

He does not take his eyes off the righteous; he enthrones them with kings and exalts them forever.

Job 36:7

#growthroom

At the start of the school year, when I bought school uniform for my children, I made sure I didn't buy their exact size. There had to be a little growth room.

Initially, those clothes may not have fit perfectly and at times my girls would moan about them being a bit big, but I knew that by the end of the school year they'll be more than ready for an even bigger size.

Our Father, God, wants us to be content in the life he calls us to. Sometimes we look and think, I'll never be able to measure up, but we need to give ourselves the room to grow into the life he has given us.

Be patient with yourself today.

Thank you, Father, for being patient with me.

But continue to grow in the grace and knowledge of our Lord and Saviour Jesus Christ.

2 Peter 3:18
(GNT)

#onethingafteranother

Over the past three weeks my car has been in and out of the mechanic's garage four times. This morning, when another warning light came on, I was telling my husband how frustrating it had been, one thing after the other.

Thankfully, God gave me a different picture of how our lives are full of one thing after another of his love and mercy. You see, the Bible says, God loads us with benefits daily [2]. Every day is full of one goodness after another for us to enjoy. Choose, today, not to allow anything to obscure your view of God's goodness.

Thank you, Lord, for filling my life with good.

Out of the fullness of his grace he has blessed us all, giving us one blessing after another.

John 1:16 (GNT)

#nosuchthingasafreelunch

We've all heard the saying, 'There is no such thing as a free lunch.' In other words, there is always a price to be paid, and it is not always money! For instance, you are blessed with a baby but now you have sleepless nights and endless nappy changes; you are blessed with the house of your dreams but now you must own the maintenance.

The secret, as with most things, is learning balance; not focusing too much on the price that you completely lose sight of the enjoyment of the lunch.

As you go about your day, remember you are blessed, so be responsible.

Thank you, Father, for the wisdom to be responsible with the blessings you've given me.

Much is required from those to whom much is given, for their responsibility is greater.

**Luke 12:48
(TLB)**

#tomorrow

What is it with us human beings that we can face impossibility, be offered a solution but choose to put it off till tomorrow? In Exodus chapter 8 we read about the plague of frogs. Given the choice as to when the plague should stop, "Tomorrow," Pharaoh said.

God is the God of now as much as of yesterday and tomorrow, but I pray today that we do not procrastinate till tomorrow that which we really should be doing today.

Dear Father, thank you for helping me get done today what I really need to.

I hasten and do not delay to keep your commandments.

Psalm 119:60
(ESV)

#doneapoo

"I done a poo," was the saying of one sweet toddler. With that, she was admitting she had dirtied her nappy and had the expectation she would be cleaned up.

There is something about getting older though, we often try to hide rather than admit to what we have done. It is pointless trying to hide though. The stench of your sin will find you out.

Admitting we have messed up is best. It is the first step to being fully restored.

Thank you, Lord Jesus, that I can depend on you to forgive

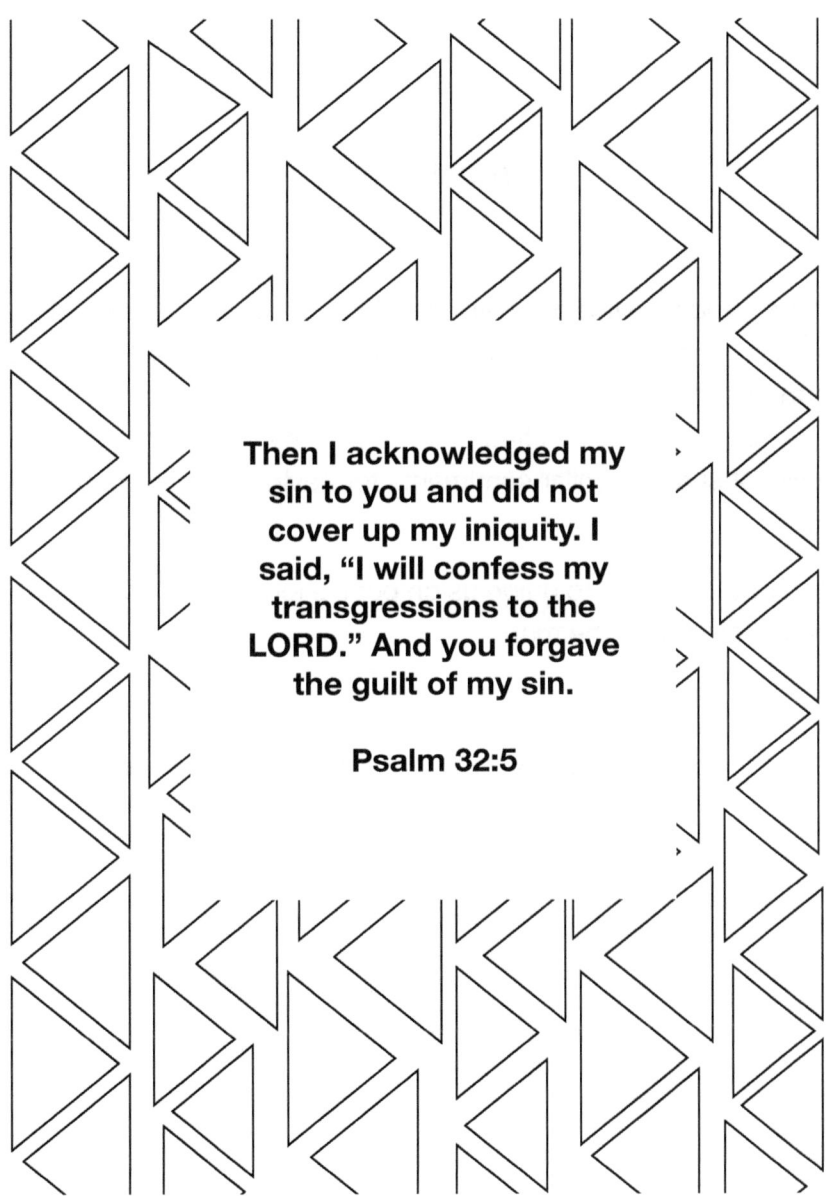

Then I acknowledged my sin to you and did not cover up my iniquity. I said, "I will confess my transgressions to the LORD." And you forgave the guilt of my sin.

Psalm 32:5

#earthmap

Some people have a general idea which direction they should be travelling and so could easily find their way should they forget to take a map. Others, though, need a map, satnav or anything else that will help them find their way. In the verse for today, the psalmist shared similar sentiments for navigating his journey on Earth.

God has promised to guide us on our life journey. As you set out today, remember the map.

Thank you, Father, for your word which directs me every day.

I am but a pilgrim here on earth: how I need a map— and your commands are my chart and guide.

**Psalm 119:19
(TLB)**

#beautyisintheeyeofthebeholder

With tears streaming down their face and snot running down their nose, "ewww," is the expression of most, but not you. You cuddle, kiss and try to comfort. Despite all, that's your baby and no one is going to tell you otherwise!

Guess what? Despite our flaws and short-comings God has adopted us each as his child through Jesus Christ and chosen us to be holy and blameless in his sight.

Walk in the knowledge, today, that your Heavenly Father loves you and no one can tell him to do otherwise.

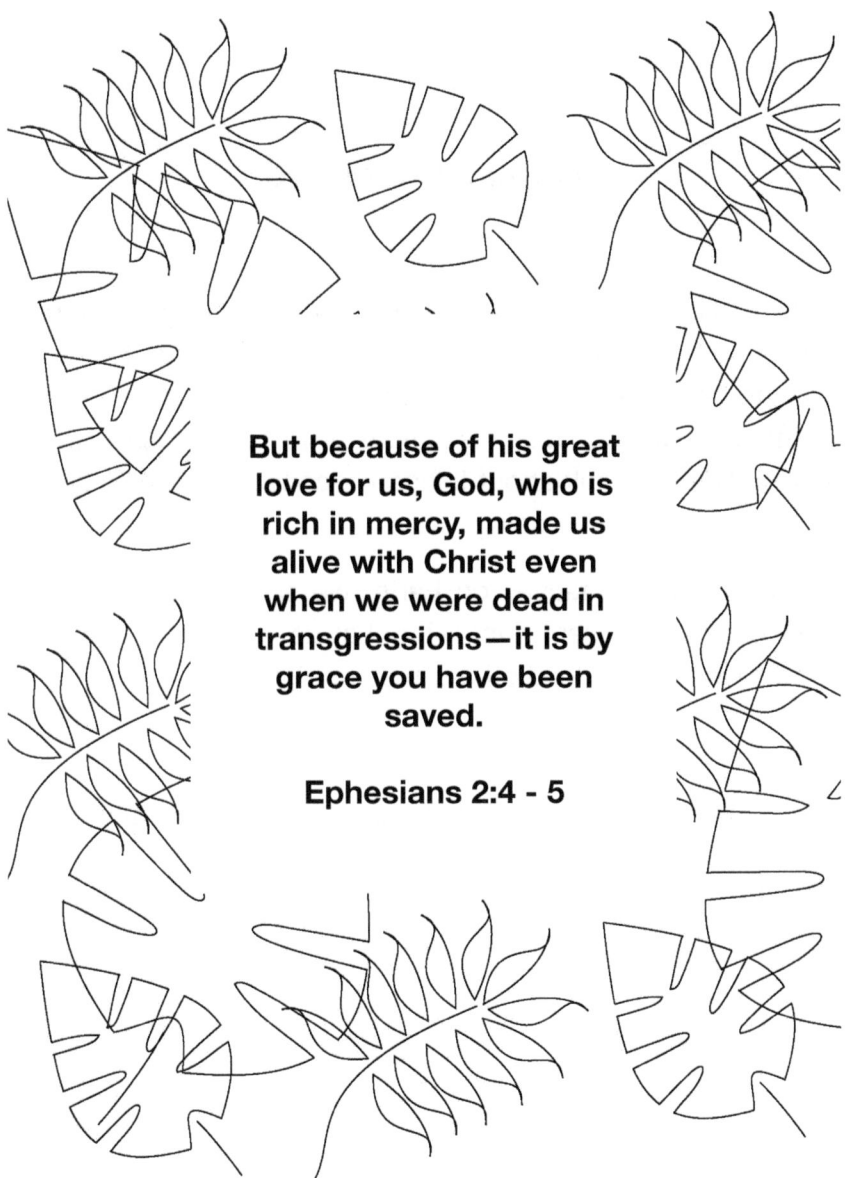

But because of his great love for us, God, who is rich in mercy, made us alive with Christ even when we were dead in transgressions—it is by grace you have been saved.

Ephesians 2:4 - 5

#againstthecrowd

In 2015, a banker was sentenced to 14 years in jail, the first person to be jailed over the fixing of a key interest rate. He didn't claim to have been falsely accused but he did claim he was being made a scapegoat as his actions were common practice. It really made me think about things we consider to be okay just because 'everyone' is doing them.

As God's representatives on Earth, we should not follow the crowd to misrepresent right living. Let us instead be the trend setters who always lead others in doing right.

Thank you, Lord, for helping me do what is right.

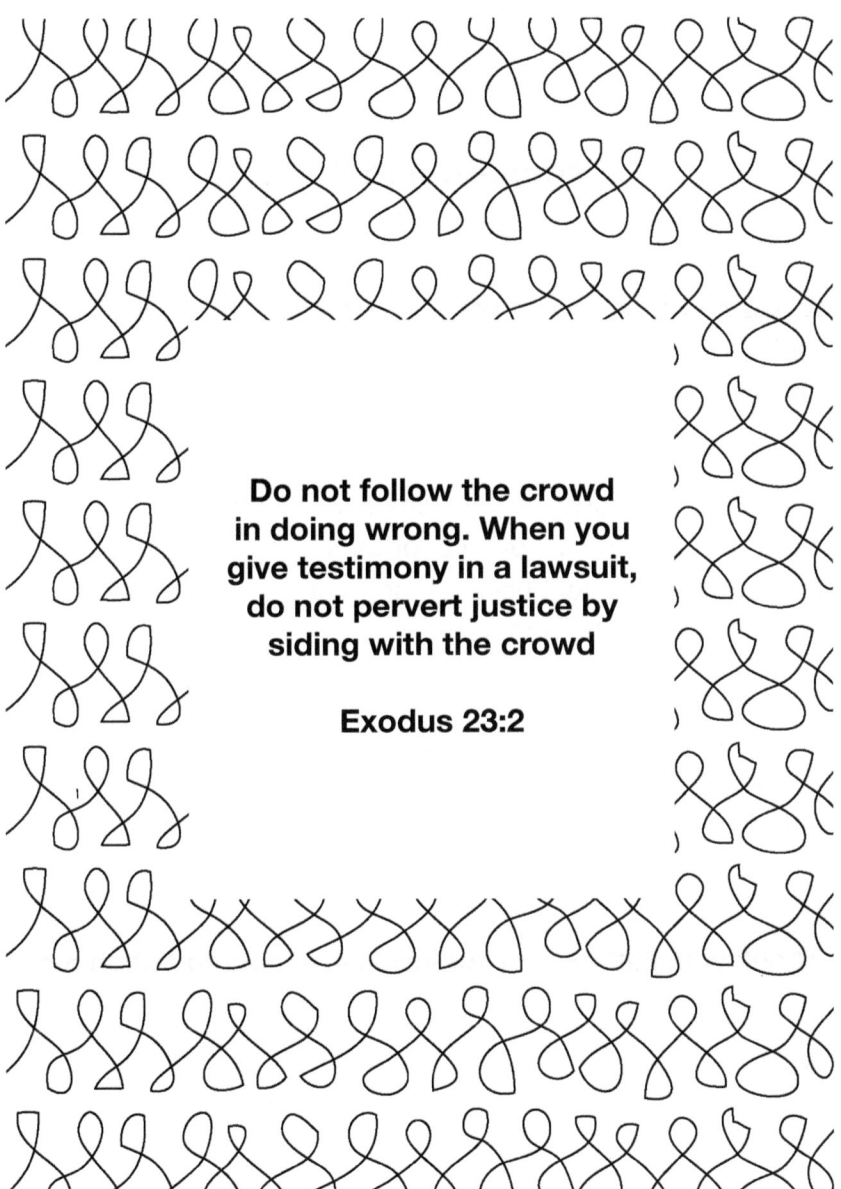

Do not follow the crowd in doing wrong. When you give testimony in a lawsuit, do not pervert justice by siding with the crowd

Exodus 23:2

#generoustoafault

My dad was often accused of being generous to a fault. He really didn't have the heart to see anyone go without and would give at his own expense, and ours, his family, we sometimes thought too.

Good on Dad though, he was simply imitating God, the Father. God's heart was so full of love for us that he could not bear us going without. He sent his best, at great cost to himself, so we may have all that the Son has.

You may already be described and even accused, of being generous to a fault. Continue in your good work, for you will be rewarded. Some of us, though, need to decide to be more generous. God loves the generous because that is his nature.

Thank you, Father, for your lavish love poured out on me.

**Generous to a fault,
you lavish your favor on
all creatures**

**Psalm 145:16
(MSG)**

#notinournature

When we think of birds we think of flying. It is in their nature to fly. We don't think of birds wallowing in mud, for that is not in their nature.

The Bible makes us understand that it is not in the nature of those born into God's family to make a practice of sinning. The life of a child of God is a life that can't be comfortable wallowing in sin.

There may be something you are doing which is not really in your true nature as God's child. Acknowledging that to be the case is a great place to be. As you confess it to your loving and forgiving Father, he has promised to cleanse you and set you right with him, so you can keep on living your true nature.

Thank you, Father, for setting in me the nature of Jesus.

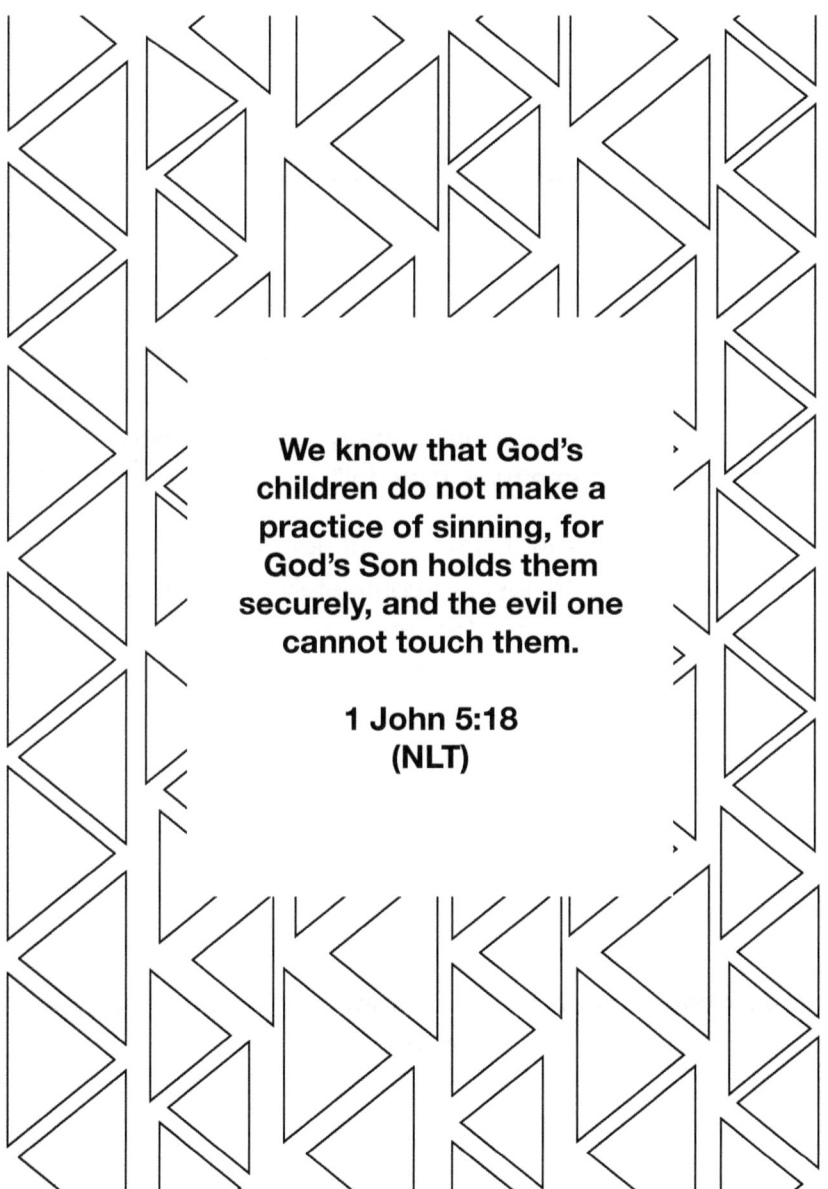

> We know that God's children do not make a practice of sinning, for God's Son holds them securely, and the evil one cannot touch them.
>
> **1 John 5:18 (NLT)**

#butmyfriendscan

There were several occasions, when my girls were growing up, where I wouldn't permit something and in a frustrated attempt to change my mind, they'd say, "But everyone in my class can." My response to that was usually, "But you are not everyone and cannot live by the same rules they do!"

As Christians, we are in this world but not of it. The rules of the world, how they do things, are completely different from those of the family we belong to. The world may live an undisciplined life and seemingly get away with it. We, however, will not get away with it. Our Father, who made the house rules, loves us too much to let us get away with it.

Let me encourage you, decide to live by the rules of the house of God.

Thank you, Lord, that your commands are all beneficial to me.

#selah

Scattered through the Book of Psalms, is this word, 'Selah'. It means to pause. Today, before we begin to rush about, before we start on resolving issues left over from yesterday, before we set about anything, let us pause and remind ourselves of who our Father, God, is.

The Lord is a great God, the great King of all gods. He controls the formation of the depths of the earth and the mightiest mountains; all are his. He made the sea and formed the land; they too are his.

The Lord's is the greatness and the power
   and the glory and the majesty and the splendor,
   for everything in heaven and earth is his.
The Lord's is the kingdom;
   He is exalted as head over all [3].

Our great and mighty Father, God, is with us at the onset and throughout our day.

Pause through your day and remember him.

Dear God, I think of your greatness and thank you for being my Father.

The Lord has made the heavens his throne; from there he rules over everything that there is.

**Psalm 103:19
(TLB)**

#whatwouldlovedo

Several years ago, some Christians wore wristbands inscribed 'WWJD' (What Would Jesus Do?). I understand the thought behind it but seeing as Jesus summarised the commandments as loving God and loving our neighbour, I personally think a more relevant question is, what would love do?

Love is very patient and kind, never jealous or envious, never boastful or proud, never haughty or selfish or rude. Love does not demand its own way. It is not irritable or touchy. It does not hold grudges and will hardly even notice when others do it wrong. It is never glad about injustice, but rejoices whenever truth wins out. If you love someone, you will be loyal to him no matter what the cost. You will always believe in him, always expect the best of him, and always stand your ground in defending him [4].

What would love do today?

Thank you, Jesus, that your love is poured into my heart, so I can love like you do.

Whoever does not love does not know God, because God is love.

1 John 4:8

#sleepinglions

When my girls were younger, and I wanted some peace and quiet, I would encourage them to play the game 'Sleeping Lions' and they would lie as still and quiet as possible. Journeying through life, we all face situations where there are what we consider lions and we would rather they were sleeping, harmless ones.

When Saul was pursuing David, we read, in 1 Samuel 26:12 (The Message Bible), *"No one woke up! They all slept through the whole thing. A blanket of deep sleep from God had fallen on them"*. God kept David safe by making those who were after him sleep.

We don't need to be afraid, our God is in the business of taming the lions we face; sending them to sleep, blinding them or whatever is required so we can get a safe passage. Trust God to do just that for you today.

Thank you, Father, that you are in the business of taming lions.

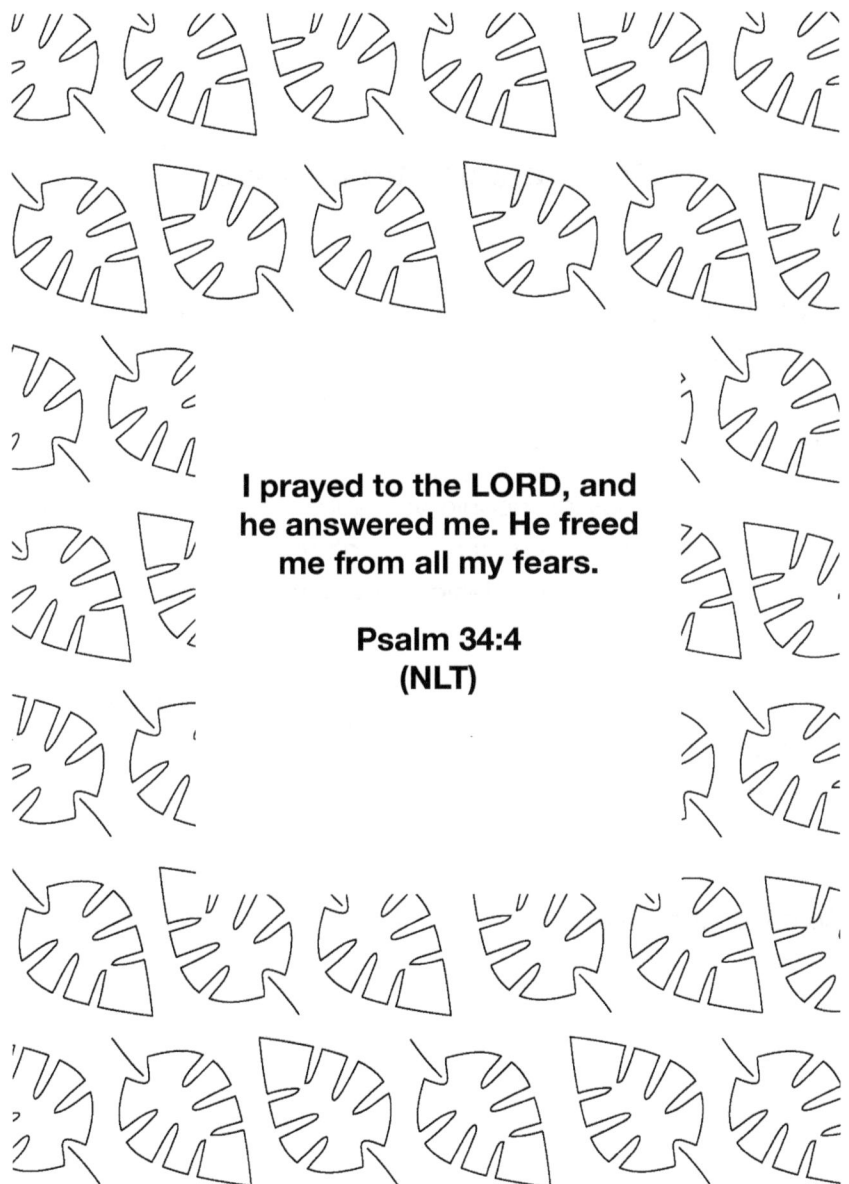

I prayed to the LORD, and he answered me. He freed me from all my fears.

Psalm 34:4 (NLT)

#feelthefearbutdoitanyway

I was speaking to my friend, telling her how I admired her public speaking skills and commented how she never appeared afraid when delivering a speech. Her response surprised me, "I do feel the fear, but I do it anyway."

Like me, there may be people you admire, strutting their stuff and presume they have no fear. Very often, though, they do feel the fear, it's just they have decided it will not stop them from doing what they need to.

There may be things that cause us to fear but we need to be those people who will not allow those things to stop us from fulfilling what we are called to do.

Go on, do it anyway!

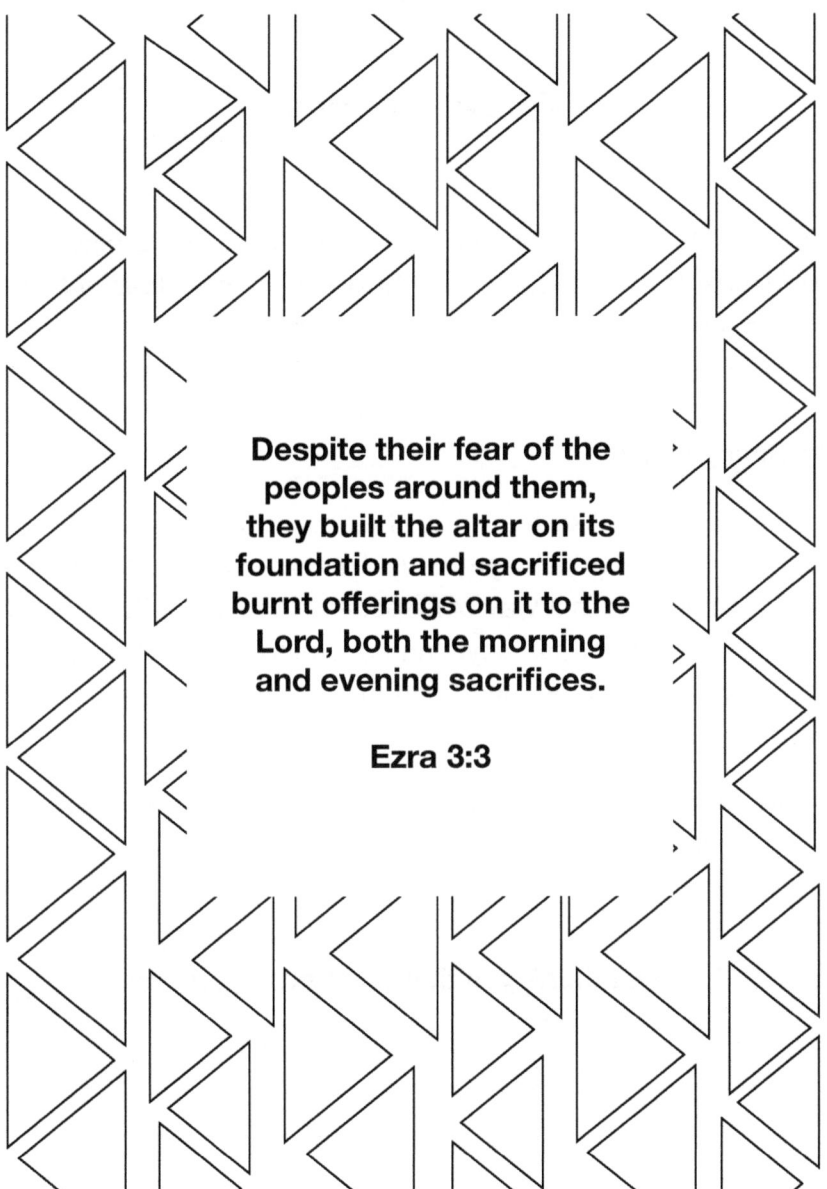

Despite their fear of the peoples around them, they built the altar on its foundation and sacrificed burnt offerings on it to the Lord, both the morning and evening sacrifices.

Ezra 3:3

#didyouhearme

Picture a little boy asking his mum if he can go out to play with his friends. It seems she did not hear him for she does not answer immediately, continuing with task she is doing. He waits a few seconds and concludes she must not have heard. So, he asks again, a tad louder. "I heard you the first time", she starts off. Strange, that!

Sometimes I feel like that child. I've asked Father God about something and I figure he probably didn't hear because it seems he's done nothing in a way of response. Thankfully, God's word tells me whenever I ask anything according to his will I can be confident he heard me, and I can trust at just the right time he will do what is best.

Whatever you have asked God recently, his actions may appear to contradict it, but trust he heard you loud and clear.

Father, I thank you that you have heard me.

And this is the confidence that we have toward him, that if we ask anything according to his will he hears us.

1 John 5:14 (ESV)

#exitdoor

In the UK and in several other countries, building regulations make it mandatory to have emergency exit doors in buildings. When you enter a public building (especially for the first time) you would usually be made aware of the location of the exit doors. In life though, the location of exit doors is not always obvious.

In Genesis 21, we read about Hagar and Ishmael in the desert without water. For some reason, which we are not told, Hagar does not see the well which was in her vicinity. God opens her eyes to it after she and her son cry out to him.

To every problem we face there is an exit, a way out. Like Hagar, we may have to cry out to God before we see it, but we can be sure it is there and trust he will show us where.

Dear Father, thank you that I can trust you to guide me through every trial.

No trial has overtaken you that is not faced by others. And God is faithful: He will not let you be tried beyond what you are able to bear, but with the trial will also provide a way out so that you may be able to endure it.

1 Corinthians 10:13 (NET)

#havealittlepatience

Imagine a hysterical baby, crying because they are hungry. Their mum has just finished getting food ready but until that child quietens, they really can't get the food they are crying for.

We are sometimes like that child, a little frantic and hysterical in situations we face. What we really need is to calm down and give God time. His intentions are good towards us, and if we would have a little patience we would see that he does just as he said he would.

Have patience and confidence in God.

**Thank you, Father, I don't need to stress out.
You are actively working for my good.**

I waited patiently for the Lord;
And He inclined to me,
And heard my cry.
He also brought me up out of a horrible pit,
Out of the miry clay,
And set my feet upon a rock,
And established my steps.

Psalm 40:1-2

#misrepresented

Have you ever been misrepresented? The frustration, for example, of someone incorrectly recounting something you said! Jesus was frustrated with the Pharisees and teachers of the law for misrepresenting him before the people. Just like us, Jesus cares about us portraying him correctly.

Double check the facts of God's word. Is your life correctly representing Jesus?

Dear Father, thank you for teaching me to know and represent you well.

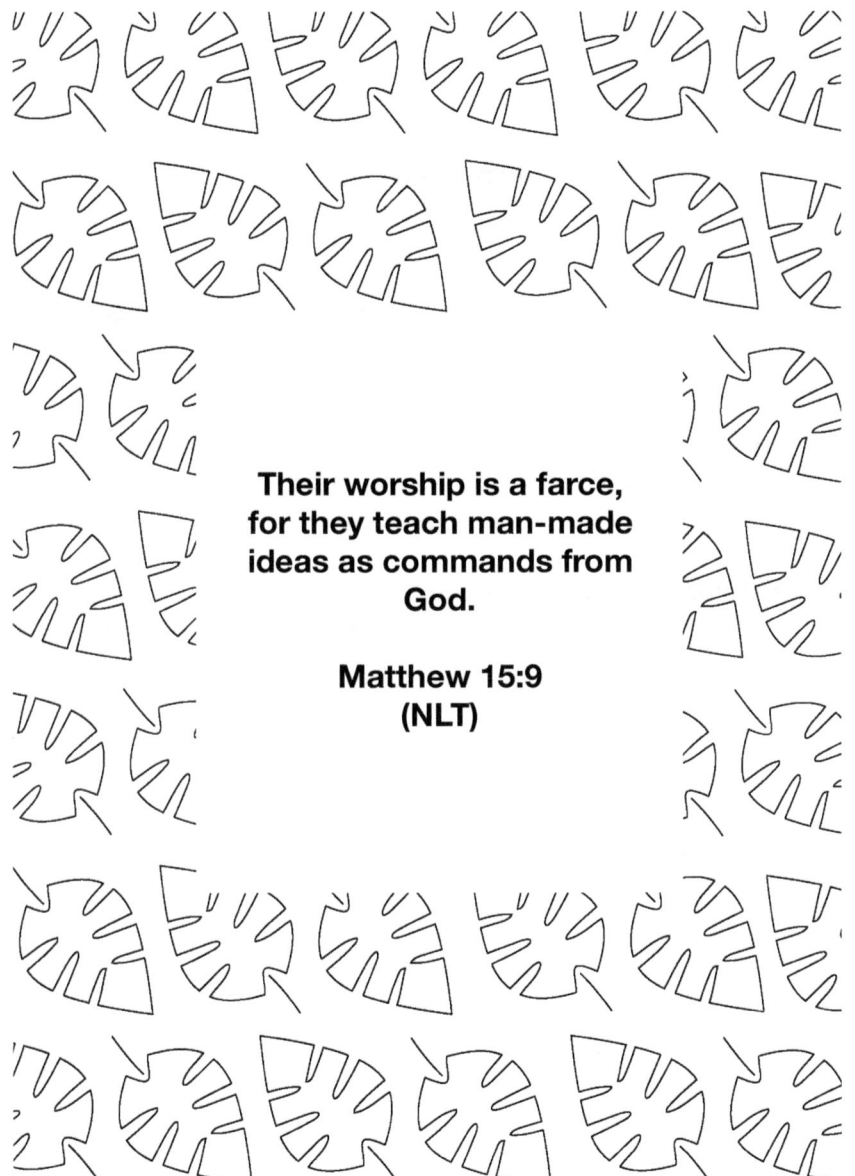

Their worship is a farce, for they teach man-made ideas as commands from God.

Matthew 15:9
(NLT)

#morethan

God always does more than enough. He lavishes, pours out and, in fact, Ephesians 3:20 talks of him doing exceedingly abundantly above what we ask of him. So, when in Matthew 5:47 Jesus asks, *"... what are you doing more than others?"* I can understand the basis for the question. He is, in effect, saying, be like your Father, doing more than the norm.

In everything you do, be the one who does more than is expected. In conversations, for example, be the one who compliments and encourages the most. Seek out ways today to be more like Jesus.

Thank you, Jesus, for being my example to follow.

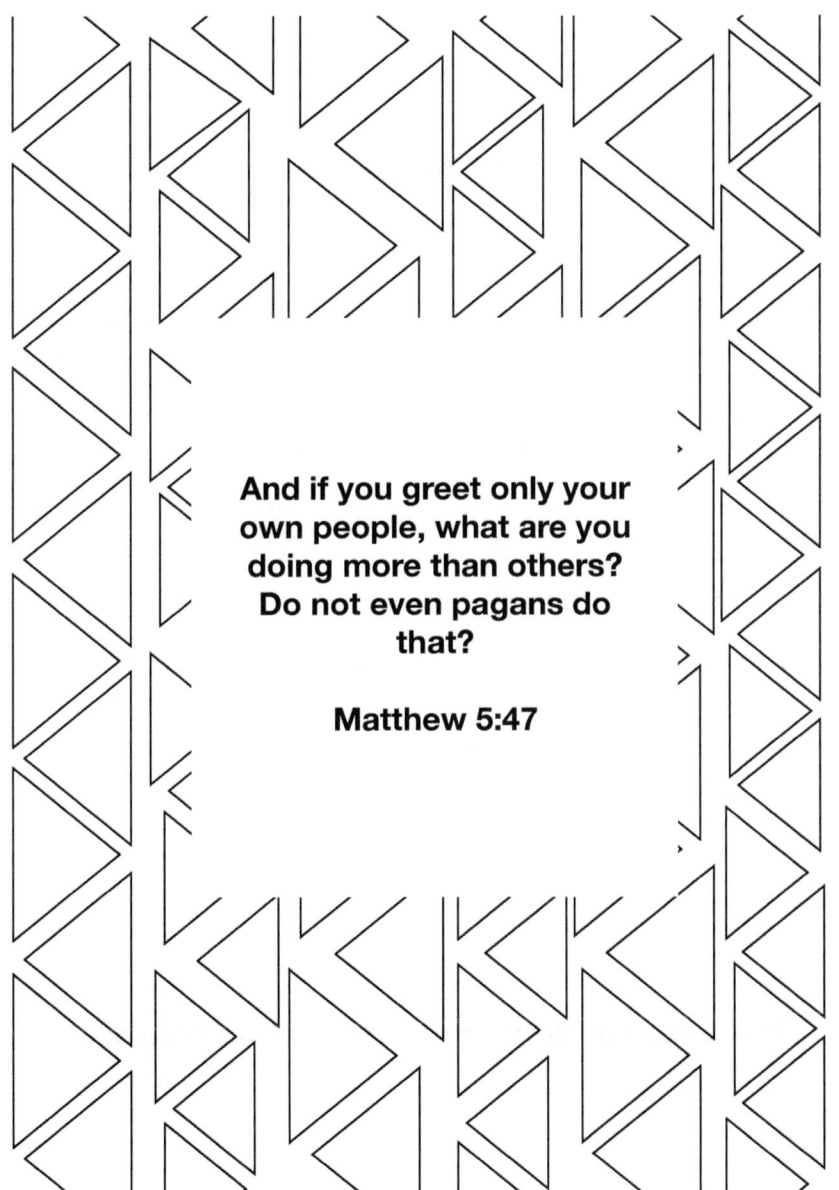

And if you greet only your own people, what are you doing more than others? Do not even pagans do that?

Matthew 5:47

#stillhere

Babies want to be near their mother to feel safe. That's why you'd often find them soothed in her arms. But as the child grows older, Mum must train the child to know she is still there, even when out of sight, and the child is safe.

It's a gradual training; learning to sleep in their own bed, learning to be left in the sitting room whilst Mum fixes dinner, learning to be left at nursery and so on.

God, the Father, wants mature sons and daughters and so trains us that though we may not feel his presence, he (as he said) is there always. The question is, will you mature to believe the Father's promise?

Act, today, in the confidence you are never alone, God is with you!

Thank you Father the confidence of your presence.

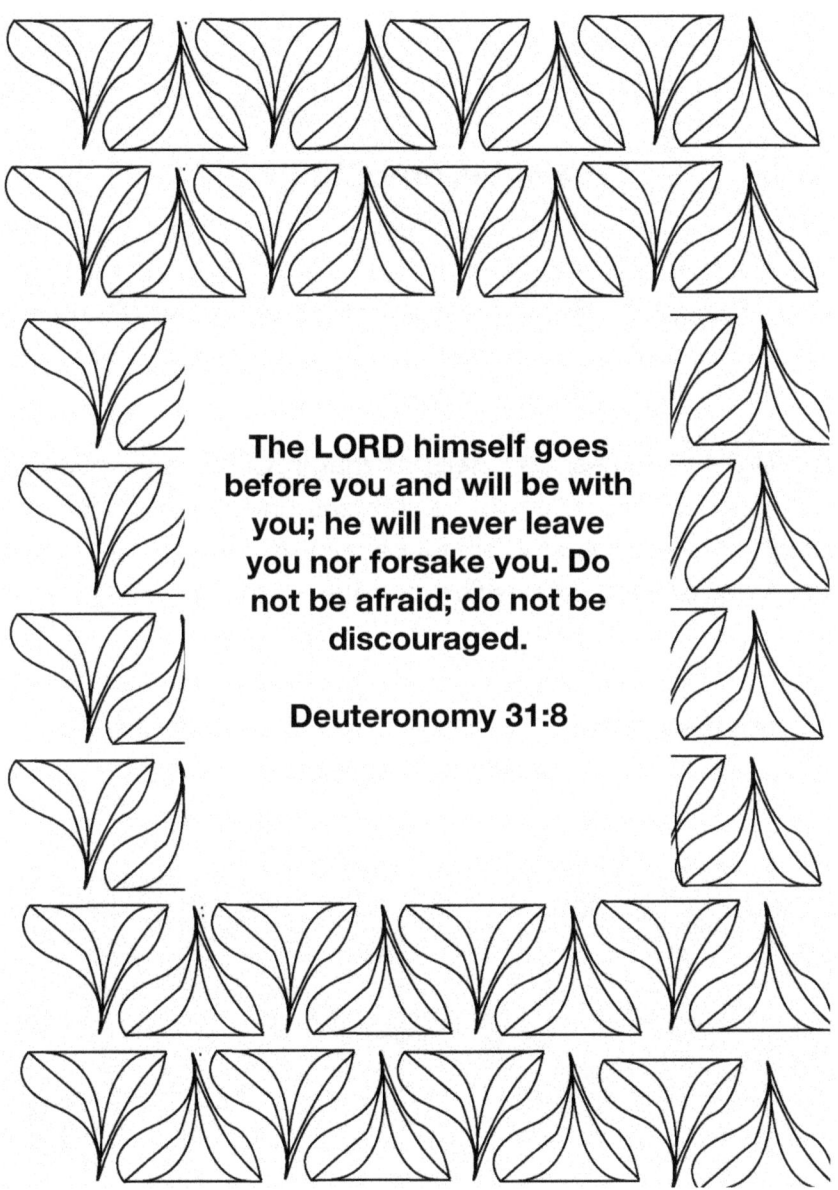

The LORD himself goes before you and will be with you; he will never leave you nor forsake you. Do not be afraid; do not be discouraged.

Deuteronomy 31:8

#viewfromuphigh

When flying, I do love looking out of the window of the plane to see massive trucks on the ground appear as tiny ants as we ascend. Everything is smaller from a height.

The Bible, in Ephesians [5], tells us that in Christ Jesus we are positioned in the highest of heights, the place of authority and power. The massive problem I face right now is really a tiny ant when viewed from my position in Jesus.

Dear Jesus, thank you that in you I am seated above any problem I may face.

Who is like the Lord our God, the One who sits enthroned on high, who stoops down to look on the heavens and the earth?

Psalm 113:5-6

#whatsthatsmell

Dead things stink. Think of the reactions you've seen on TV and in books of people when they come across a dead body—it really is foul!

The Bible says of us who believe in Jesus as our Lord, "Your old life is dead [6]." We are dead to the stinky life of envy, lying, cheating and the like. We are now alive with the fresh smell of new life, Jesus' life in us. No wonder people look at us and notice the sweet aroma coming from our lives. Today we can tell them, it's Jesus living in me!

Thank you, Jesus, for the fragrance of your presence in my life.

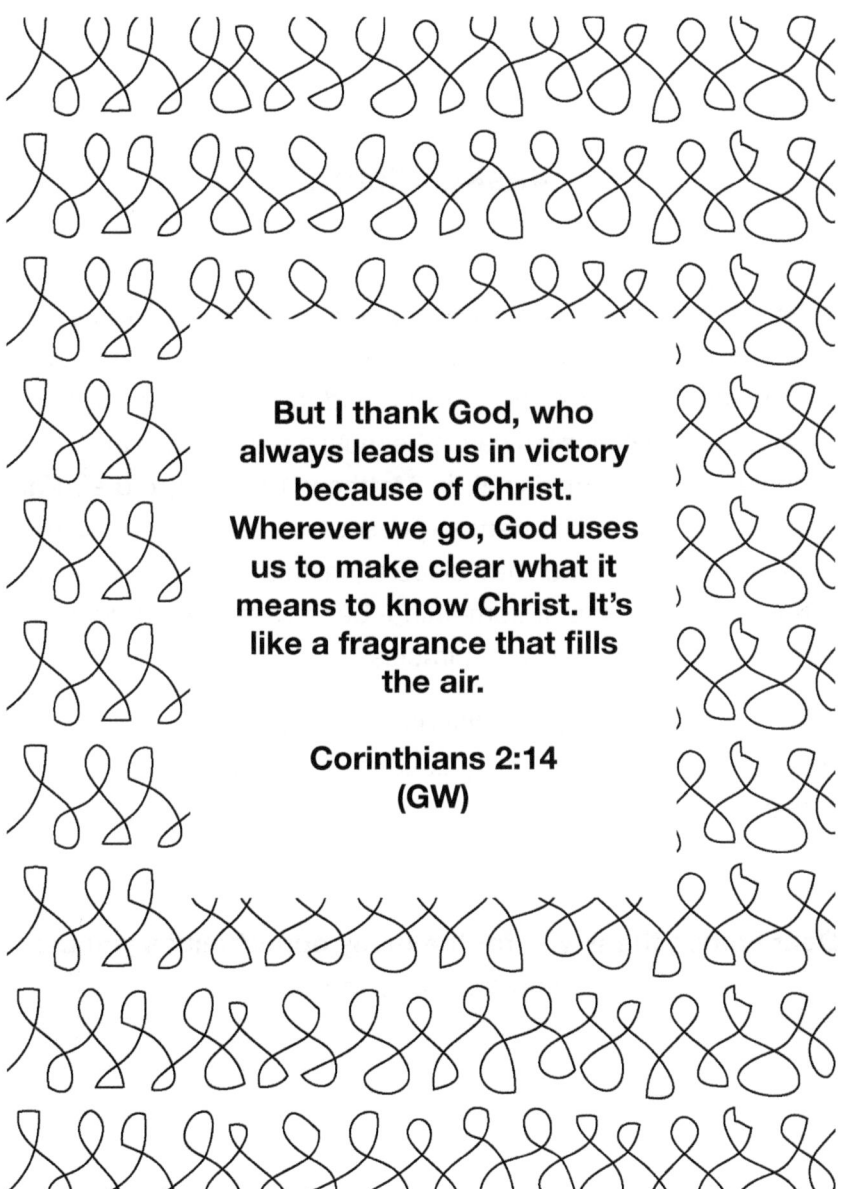

But I thank God, who always leads us in victory because of Christ. Wherever we go, God uses us to make clear what it means to know Christ. It's like a fragrance that fills the air.

Corinthians 2:14 (GW)

#askandlearn

Quite often when people do things that aren't natural to us, we explain it away. For instance, a mum meets another mum at the school gate who looks fit and trim and instead of asking how, the first mum explains it away, 'She must naturally have an active metabolism.' The Pharisees, in Matthew 12:22-24, did similar. When Jesus healed the demon-possessed man, they explained away the miracle. Had they sincerely asked Jesus how he did it, they may have learnt something, been saved and even been given the power to perform miracles.

Today, rather than explain things away based on your current understanding or belief, ask questions and make it an opportunity to learn.

Dear Father, thank you for the many opportunities you provide for me to learn.

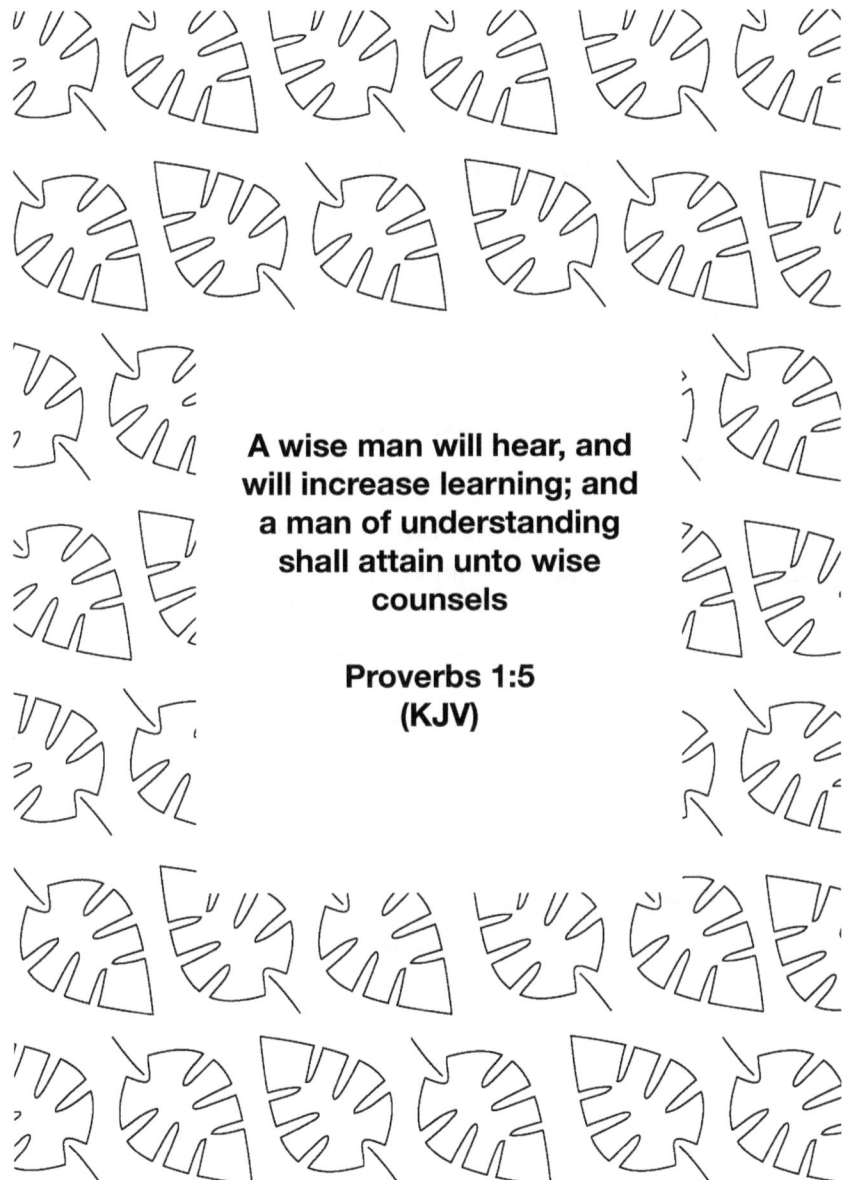

A wise man will hear, and will increase learning; and a man of understanding shall attain unto wise counsels

Proverbs 1:5 (KJV)

#betterthanideserve

"How are you?"

"Better than I deserve to be," was the response I heard my trainee give her colleague. The response made me smile but also made me think.

You see, when our focus is misplaced we may think we have reasons to complain about one thing or the other. However, when we focus on the generosity of God in pouring out his grace and not giving us what we deserve we cannot but be thankful.

Go about your day with the thought, because of Jesus you are so much better off than you should have been and be thankful.

Thank you, Jesus, for your many mercies towards me.

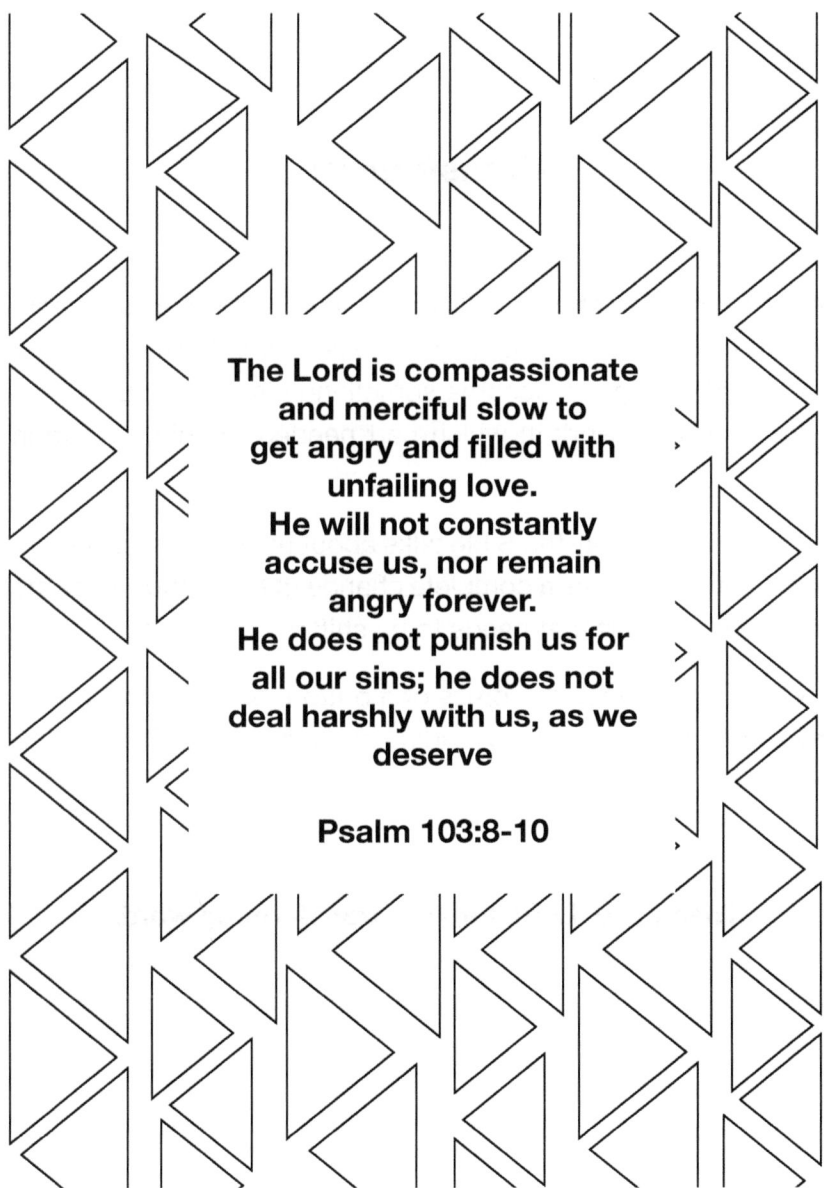

The Lord is compassionate and merciful slow to get angry and filled with unfailing love.
He will not constantly accuse us, nor remain angry forever.
He does not punish us for all our sins; he does not deal harshly with us, as we deserve

Psalm 103:8-10

#transformers

The exciting thing about the Transformers toy line was that there was more to each toy than you could immediately see. The toys could change to become something else, but you needed to know how to work it; which part needed to shift, or button pressed.

In the verse for today the Bible talks about us being transformed. God wants us to have a complete change of heart and life for the better and the part that needs to be shifted is our mind.

It will take more than the press of a button, but we can start today by spending more time reading and thinking on God's word, the Bible.

Thank you, Lord, for your transforming word.

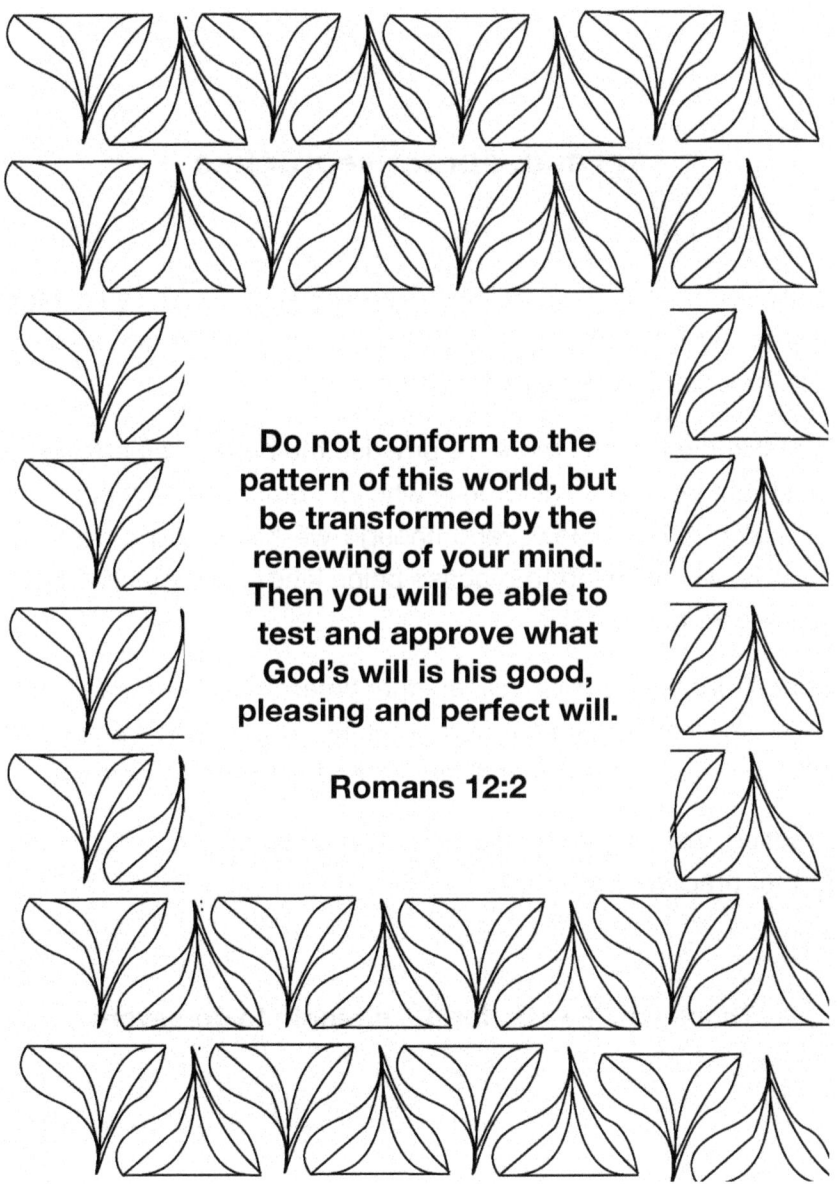

Do not conform to the pattern of this world, but be transformed by the renewing of your mind. Then you will be able to test and approve what God's will is his good, pleasing and perfect will.

Romans 12:2

#practisepractisepractise

In my work, I deliver training courses and usually end each course by encouraging the delegates to practise in order to master what they have just learnt.

We all know that the more we practise the better we get at anything, but we expect differently when it comes to spiritual things for some reason. However, although we have God's grace to help us, we still need to practise being kind, generous and hospitable, for example.

Sometimes we do very well, at other times, maybe we slack. But if we are to excel, like the child learning to walk who falters and falls, we need to pick ourselves up, and get back to practice.

Practice makes perfect so take today as an opportunity for further practise.

Thank you, Father, for the strength to persevere.

Whatever you have learned or received or heard from me, or seen in me—put it into practice. And the God of peace will be with you.

Philippians 4:9

#itwillallendintears

"One of you is going to end up crying if you don't stop the rough play," was a warning I occasionally had to give my children when they were younger. Seeing the end from the start is not always possible but I'm sure there are some situations where we've known, up front, this isn't going to end well.

Now, when you can see the end isn't going to be desirable, the sensible thing to do is change course. There may be something God has been speaking to you about and wants you to change. We are warned throughout the Bible, walking in disobedience to God's word will not end well. If you are being warned, decide to act accordingly now.

Lord, thank you for speaking to me and helping me to obey what you say.

Whoever gives heed to instruction prospers, and blessed is the one who trusts in the LORD.

Proverbs 16:20

#protected

Bodyguards are always in attendance wherever you see members of the royal family. Sometimes they are very visible and at other times less so. Regardless, should there be any hint of a commotion, you can be sure they will make their presence known; springing into action, ready to protect.

In the same way, we can be sure the King of Kings has not sent his family out without protection. Sometimes we are very aware of God's presence and protection and at other times we wonder if he is there at all. Nevertheless, we can rest in the knowledge that he is always present and watching over us.

Thank you, Father, for your protection always.

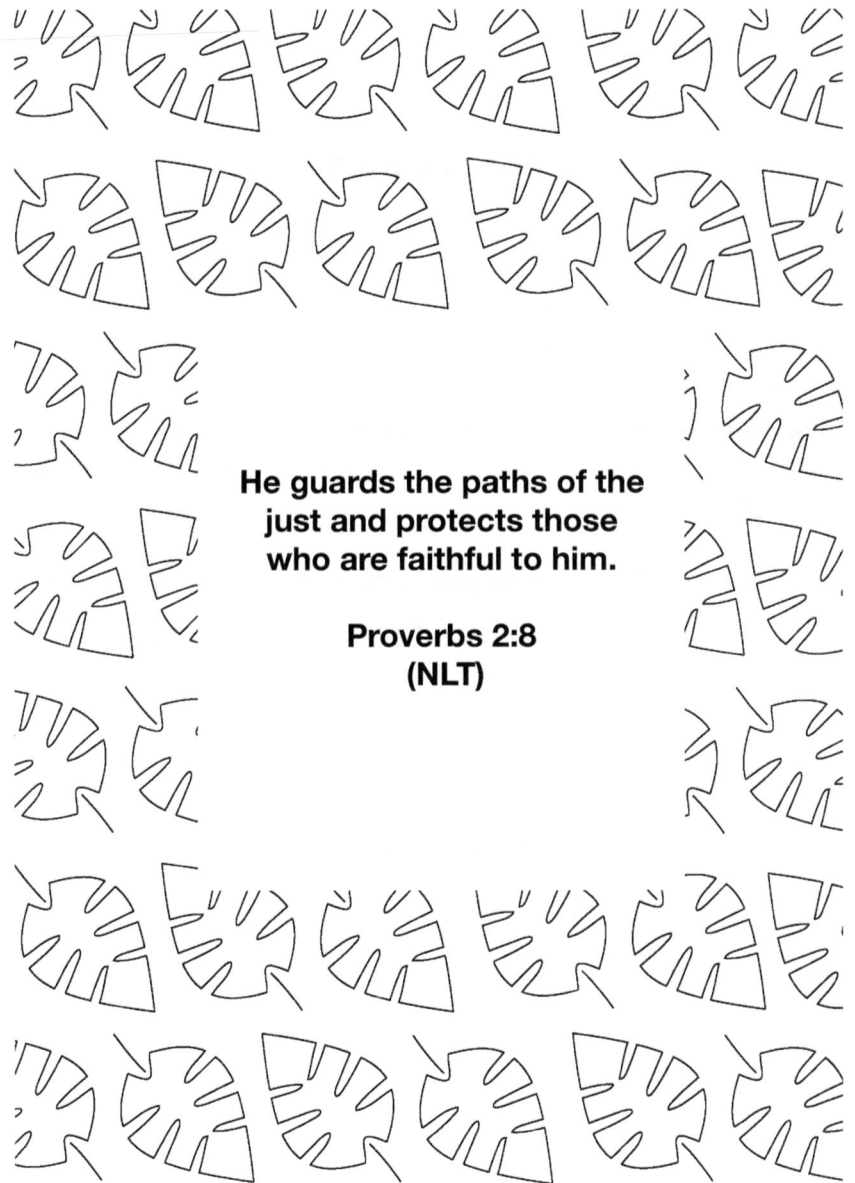

He guards the paths of the just and protects those who are faithful to him.

Proverbs 2:8 (NLT)

#youcanhaveitbothways

My friend was telling me how she really loved cake with ice cream and wished she could have it every day yet still loose the weight she wanted to. I guess she concluded that she couldn't have her cake and eat it. The truth is there aren't many scenarios where we can have it both ways except when we are living by God's word.

Give and it will be given to you, a classic example of having it both ways; we are a blessing to someone but get blessed back. Enjoy being a generous giver, knowing you will never be in lack.

Thank you, God, that you bless us as we bless others.

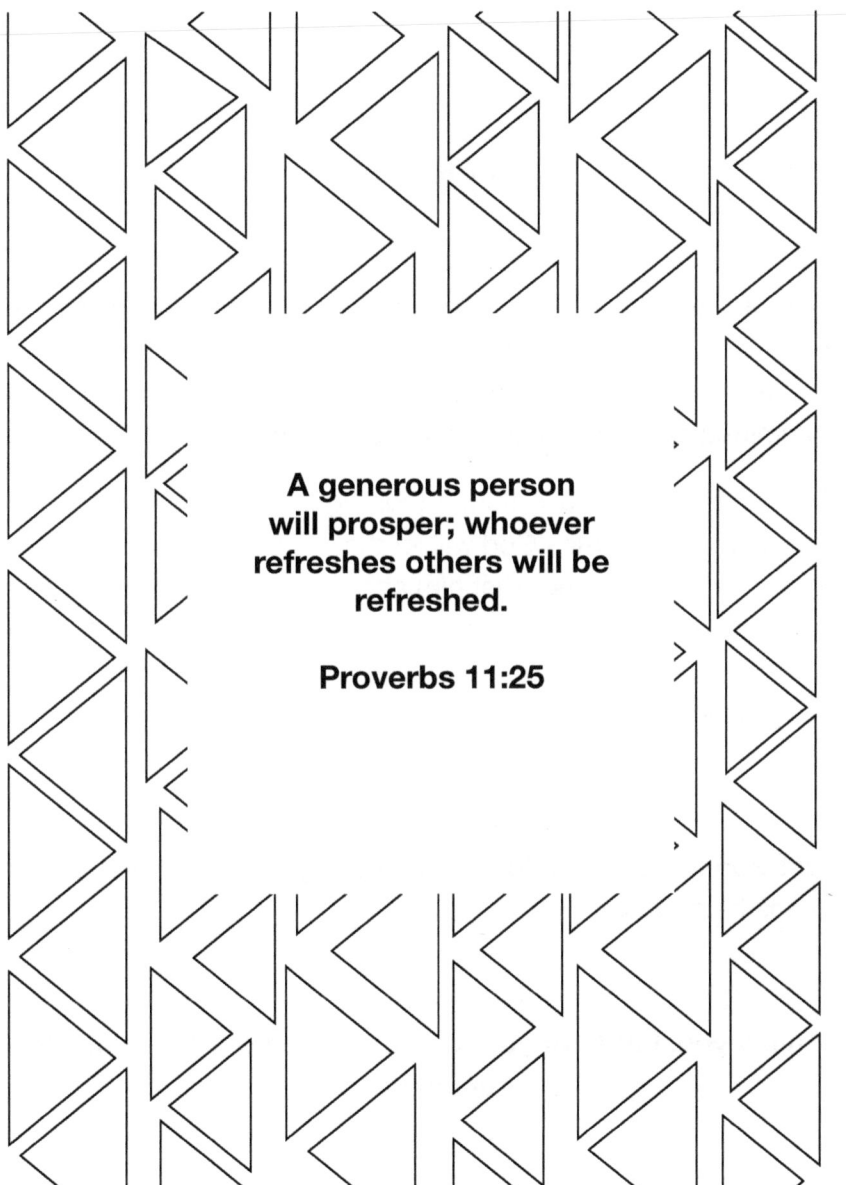

A generous person will prosper; whoever refreshes others will be refreshed.

Proverbs 11:25

#closure

I am amazed at Joseph's move from prison to palace. As we read about this in Genesis 41, there is no consideration of why Joseph was ever in prison or any putting right of the wrongs committed against him. It appears all that was ignored.

Personally, I like to see things thoroughly worked through and closed off. Sometimes God will let that be the case and at other times I have let off and trust him about it. From experience, I've learnt that if I get hung up on closing things off how I want, I end up losing out. I mean, imagine if Joseph said to Pharaoh before interpreting his dream, "Hold on, let's first deal with Potiphar's wife!"

Whatever the situation that hasn't had an expected closure, trust God in his grace, to pull you through and work things out just as he chooses.

Thank you, Lord, for your grace to see me through all circumstances.

Don't say, "I will get even for this wrong." Wait for the LORD to handle the matter.

Proverbs 20:22 (NLT)

#themanual

There is hardly any product without a manual of how it operates to get the best out of it. Sometimes I struggle with my phone and give up, thinking it can't do what I want, only for one of my daughters to show me how. I had not taken the time to read the instructions in the manual and so wasn't getting the most out of it.

Our life is too important to live outside of all we can be and do and there is no shortcut doing that. We learn some things though others by listening to preaches and teachings, but nothing takes the place of seeking out for ourselves what God has said in his manual, the Bible. So, make the decision to study God's word more.

Thank you, Father, for giving us the manual to life; your Word.

I delight in your decrees; I will not neglect your word

Psalm 119:16

#believethat

God says of himself, "I am the light of the world [7]"and generally it is no issue for us, as Christians, to believe that. God also says of you and me, "You are the light of the world." Our challenge is to believe that too!

My issue is, I look at my life and it does not always line up with what he says. This is just like a building site which does not measure up completely to the plan the architect has. The architect says, "This is the kitchen" and it really looks like a pile of rubble. Give it time though, a few blocks moved out, a few more things brought in and he was right, it really was the kitchen all the time.

So it is with each of our lives, God speaks of us as he sees us, completed. His Spirit is at work within us making us more and more like who he says we are. Today, believe and focus on all God says you are.

Father, thank you for the faith to believe what you say concerning me.

You are the light of the world--like a city on a hilltop that cannot be hidden.

Matthew 5:14 (NLT)

#prayforyourenemies

I had an issue with someone at work once and I took the situation to God in prayer. Okay, to be more honest, I was pretty much reporting the other person to God. I later listened to a preach about praying for people who had hurt us.

It is easy to pray about people but praying for people requires me to care for that person, as God does. God knows harbouring hatred will not benefit us which is why he tells us to pray for anyone who mistreats or persecutes us [8].

Trust God to work justice but do your part as commanded, pray for whoever might have hurt you.

Thank you, Lord, for giving me the grace to pray for those who have wronged me.

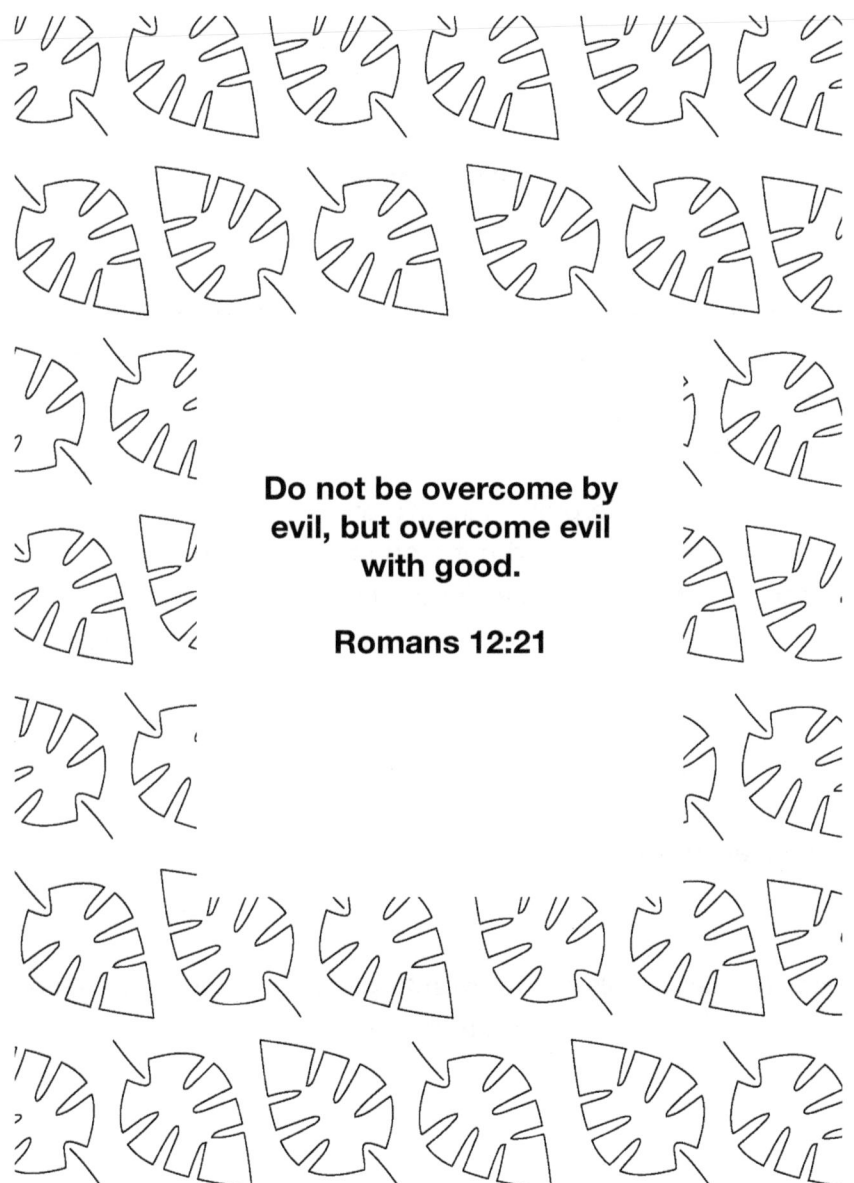

Do not be overcome by evil, but overcome evil with good.

Romans 12:21

#extramile

I'd offered my daughter an amount of money to do a specific job for me. When I came to inspect, she had not just done a thorough job but had done more than I'd asked her to. Impressed and pleased, I gave her more than we had agreed.

When called to interpret Pharaoh's dream, we read in Genesis 50:25-40 how Joseph did not stop at just that. He went on to advise on what should be done. The advice seemed wise to Pharaoh and he promoted Joseph to second in command in Egypt. Similarly, in Genesis 24, Rebekah not only gave Abraham's servant water to drink she also watered his camels. The servant saw that as answer to prayer and Rebekah became Isaac's wife. A reward always follows the one who does more so determine to be that someone.

Dear Father, thank you for granting me the wisdom to excel more at my work.

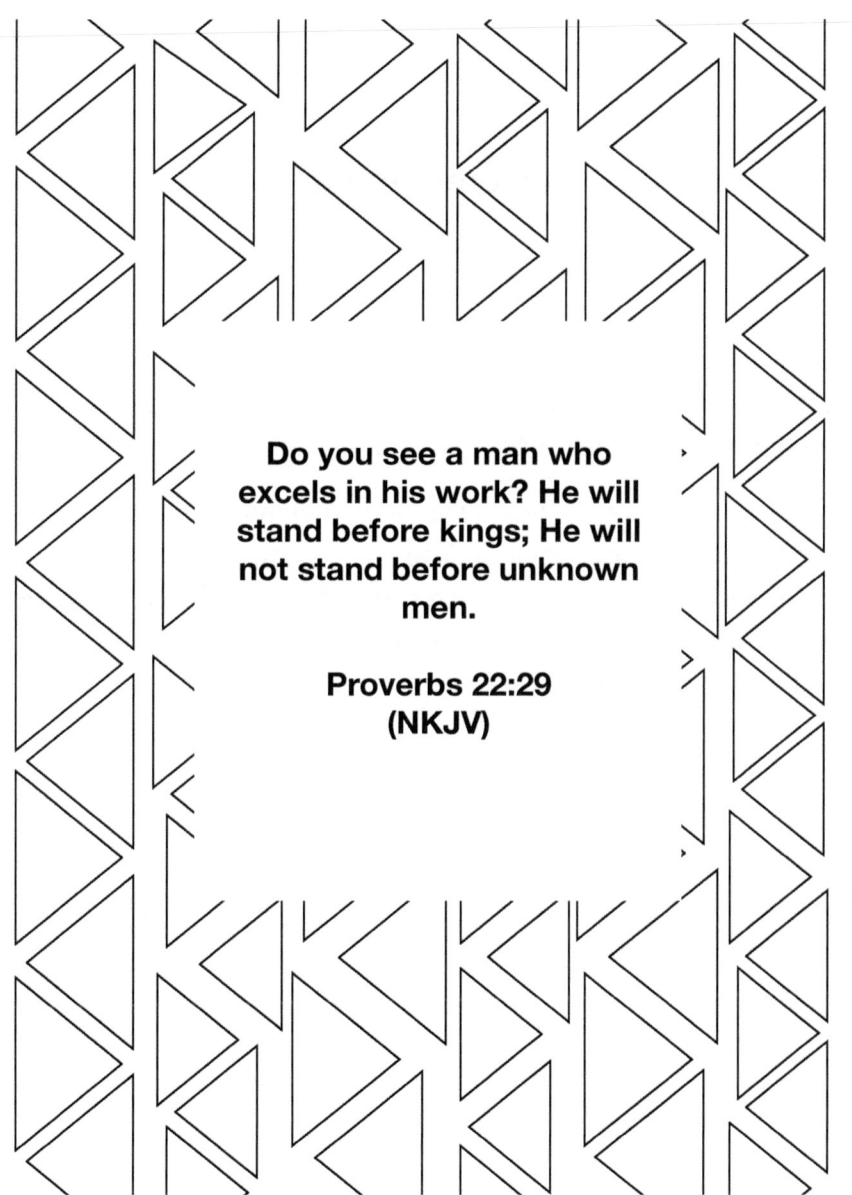

Do you see a man who excels in his work? He will stand before kings; He will not stand before unknown men.

Proverbs 22:29 (NKJV)

#secretservice

To serve or be seen, what is the motive behind all you do? Jesus, in Matthew 23:5-6, looked at the Pharisees and commented that all their works were done to be seen. They might have been serving but their motive was all wrong.

I must admit there are times I've served wanting to be noticed, recognised and appreciated. The Bible is clear, though, about whose recognition we should be seeking and therefore what our motive should be in all serving. It should all be about our love for God and wanting to please only him.

Dear Father, help me serve with the right motive always.

That your charitable deed may be in secret; and your Father who sees in secret will Himself reward you openly.

Matthew 6:4
(NKJV)

#stressbuster

It was a few days into the year and I was being asked if I'd had a stressful Christmas time, especially as the person knew I had my three brothers and their families over. My response was, "No, not really. The key is preparation. Once you do the prep beforehand, you don't have to stress the day."

I must admit I'm not always as prepared as I should be. In fact, sometimes I put it off, thinking I can get things completed successfully without. But I have learnt that putting in the prep at the right time, takes away the stress I would otherwise experience.

Whatever it is we are trying to do or achieve, wisdom will teach us that preparation is paramount and should never be procrastinated or put off.

Thank you, Father, for the wisdom to do today what will profit my tomorrow.

Without having any chief, officer or ruler, she prepares her food in summer, and gathers her sustenance in harvest

**Proverbs 6:7-8
(RSV)**

#bittersweet

It smelt horrible and tasted even worse, but my daughter was telling me she had started drinking apple cider vinegar daily. "Rather you than me," I said to her. "Yes, but if it is going to do me good …" She was willing to suffer through the unpleasant experience because she knew the benefits it would bring.

We go through hard times, some as trivial as having a bitter tasting drink and others more significant, though we are not glad for the situation itself, we often come through stronger and wiser.

You may be going through a difficult season just now but stay focused on God and trust him to work things out for his glory and your benefit.

Thank you, Father, for working good out of my difficult situations.

We can rejoice, too, when we run into problems and trials, for we know that they help us develop endurance.

Romans 5:3
(NLT)

#yesyou

You may have been guilty, as I have been, of rejecting a compliment. Maggie was admiring what I was wearing, and I started to say something about it not being that special. "You look lovely" she said again, only this time more firmly. I had to stop, smile and say, "Thank you."

It's a bit like when God told Gideon he is a mighty man of valour. Gideon responded by saying his family is very insignificant and, to top it off, he is the youngest in that family [9].

God, most certainly, does not need to hear from us what we are not when he made us. The question is, whether we will accept who he tells us we are.

Thank you, Father, that you are talking to me when you say, "You are chosen."

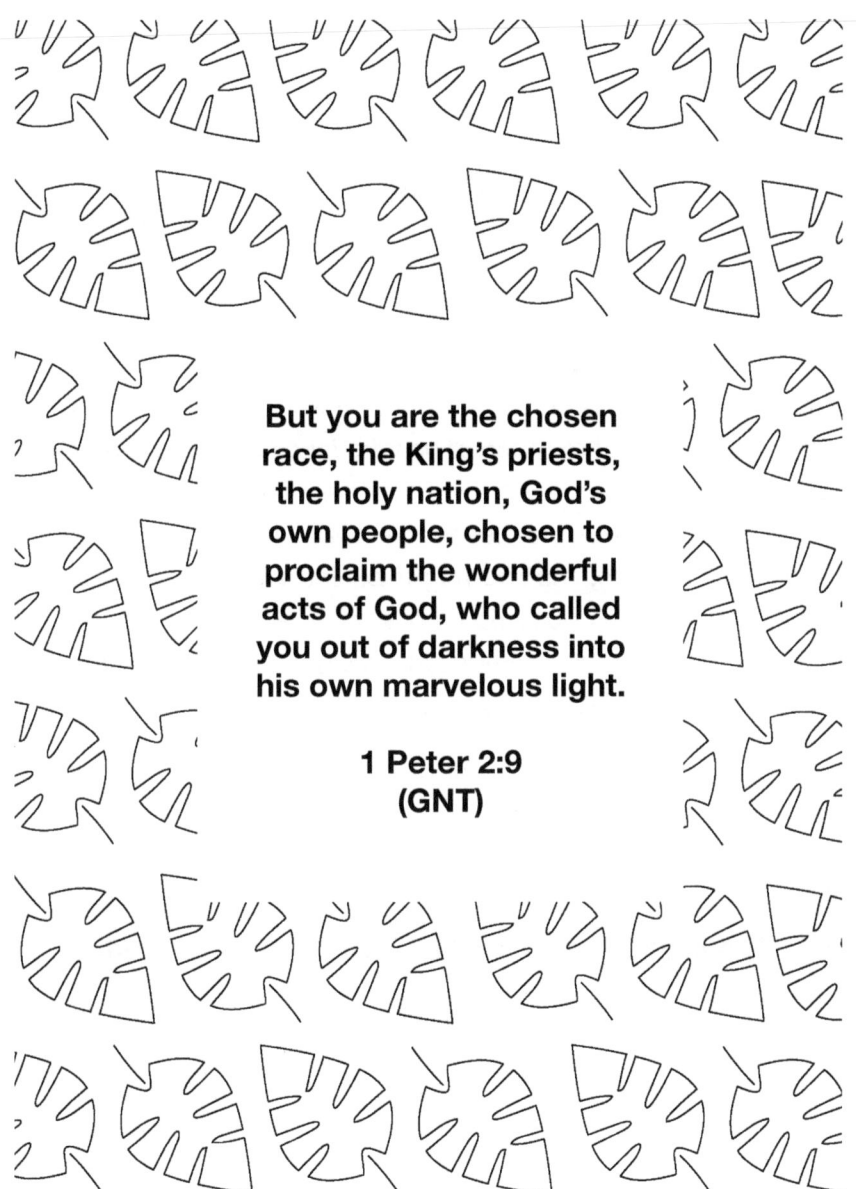

But you are the chosen race, the King's priests, the holy nation, God's own people, chosen to proclaim the wonderful acts of God, who called you out of darkness into his own marvelous light.

1 Peter 2:9
(GNT)

#Kingskid

Imagine the privilege of being born the child of an earthly monarch. Everyone who believes in Jesus has the privilege of much more. To paraphrase Romans 8:28-30 from the Phillips Bible, *we know that to those of us who love God, who are called according to his plan, everything that happens fits into a pattern for good. God, in his foreknowledge, chose us to bear the family likeness of his Son, that he might be the eldest of a family of many brothers. He chose us long ago; when the time came he called us, he made us righteous in his sight, and then lifted us to the splendour of life as his own sons.*

There isn't much else I can add to that but to say, remember who you are; the King's kid!

Thank you, Father, that in Jesus, I am your child.

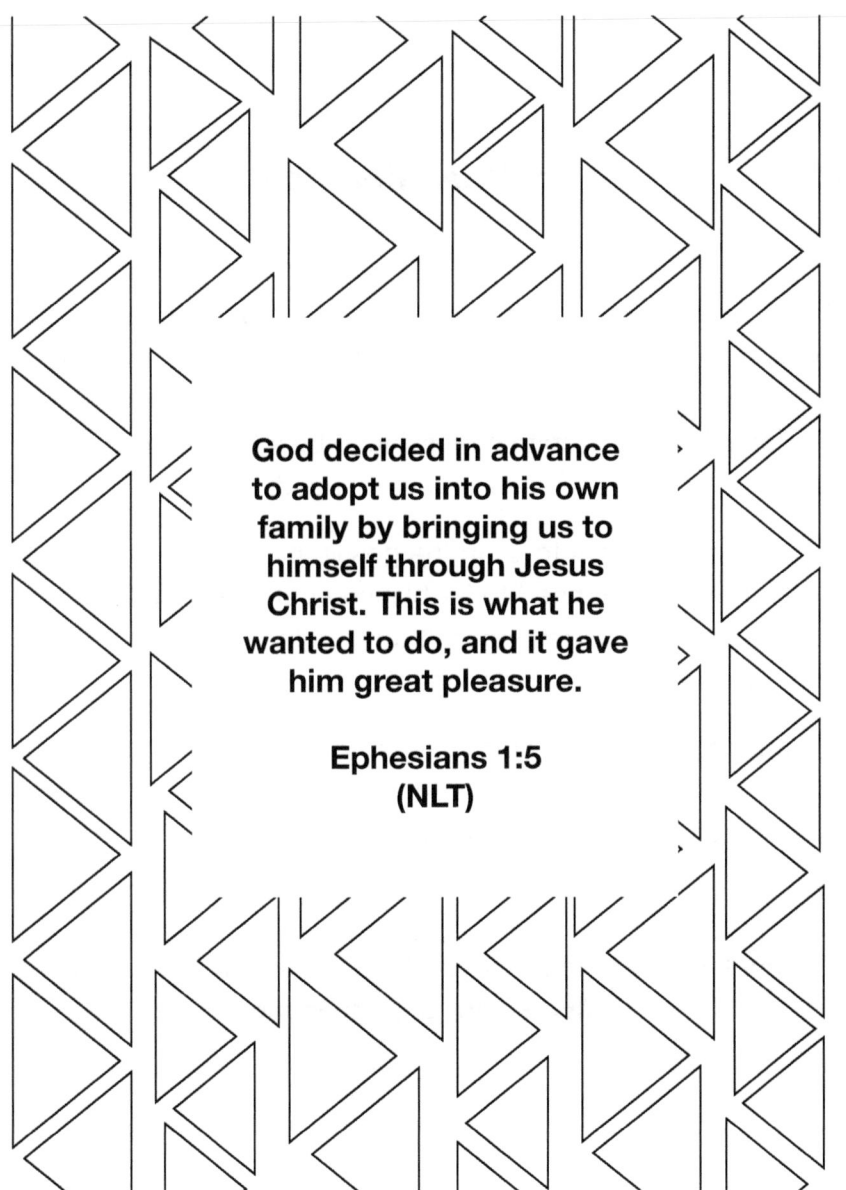

God decided in advance to adopt us into his own family by bringing us to himself through Jesus Christ. This is what he wanted to do, and it gave him great pleasure.

Ephesians 1:5 (NLT)

#spotthedifference

Have you ever played one of those 'spot the difference' games; for example, trying to work out what has changed from items in a box since you looked away? We enjoy playing the game, but it is not fun when, despite professing to be a Christian for years, people around us can't see what's changed.

If we are still content to sit in the gossip circle or our language is full of words that need to be blanked out when repeated, for example, maybe something isn't quite right. The truth is, Jesus in us will affect our character and the way we live.

We, and others must be able to see a noticeable difference in our lives since our salvation. Our decisions on how we live needs to be more reflective of the change we profess.

Thank you, Father, that you help me live in a way that reflects your change in me.

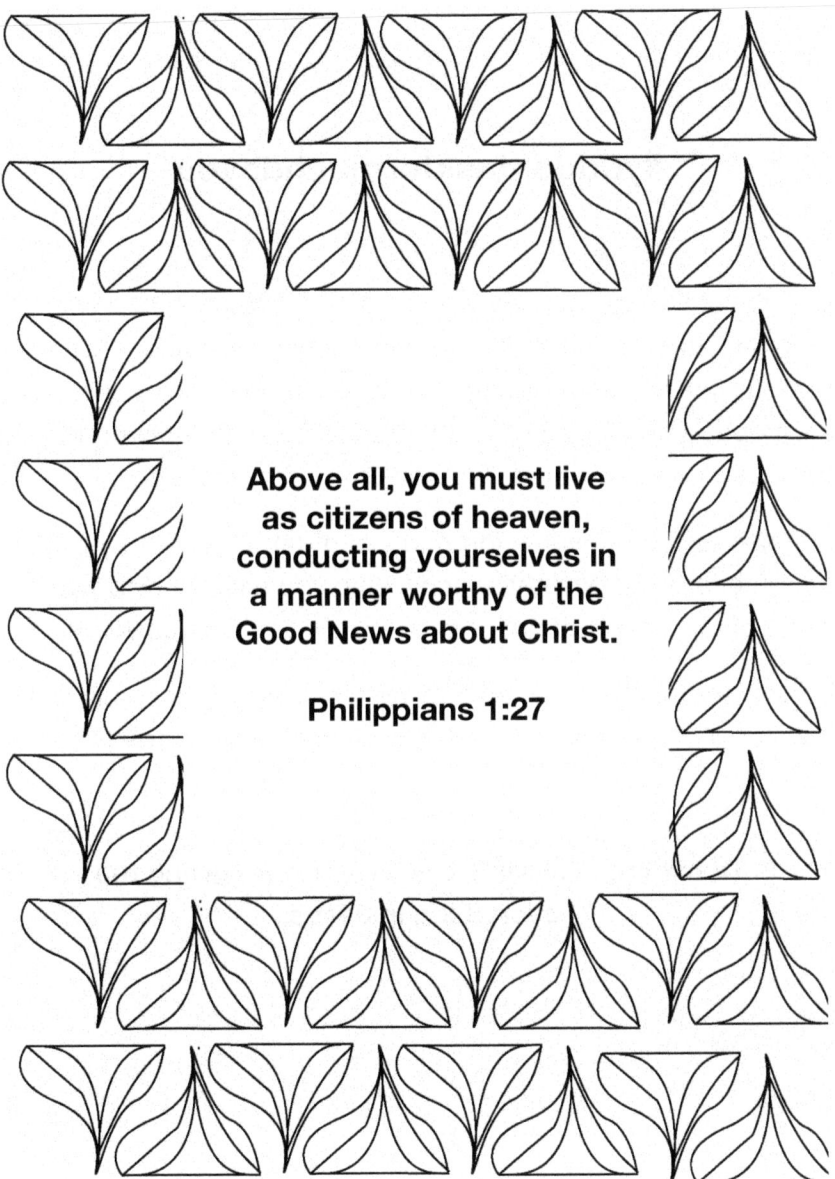

Above all, you must live as citizens of heaven, conducting yourselves in a manner worthy of the Good News about Christ.

Philippians 1:27

#youdontaskformuchdoyou

Our daughter had already asked to be picked up at 11:30pm from her late work shift. Then just before she was about to catch the bus for the start of her shift she asked if she could also be dropped off. Thinking of the round trip, of at least an hour's drive, her dad exclaimed, "You don't ask for much, do you?"

I mused at the conversation and wasn't at all surprised by our daughter asking. When you know who you are and who you are asking from, you are confident to ask for as much as you want.

Ponder today, the greatness of your heavenly Father, his great love for you, his child, and ask for as much as you need.

Thank you, Father, for loving me and giving me everything in Jesus.

Fear not, little flock; for it is your Father's good pleasure to give you the kingdom.

Luke 12:32 (KJV)

#quickuturnadvised

I do a lot of travel in my current job, often driving, and over the years I have made a few wrong turns. Before, I'd keep driving, thinking there must be a link back to the right road further on. However, that has been rather costly and so I have come to learn it is best to do a U-turn as soon as possible.

In a similar vein, it is something I'm learning in my journey with God. I find that as soon as He prompts me about a mistake, I'm best repenting, doing a U-turn, and then continuing in the right way. Ignoring that prompting and thinking I'll get to it later or even that it doesn't matter usually means I end up very far off the desired destination.

As you journey through your day, remember, a U-turn with God simply starts with acknowledging and apologising, and it is best done sooner rather than later.

Thank you, Lord, you kindly prompt and help me when I need to make a U-turn.

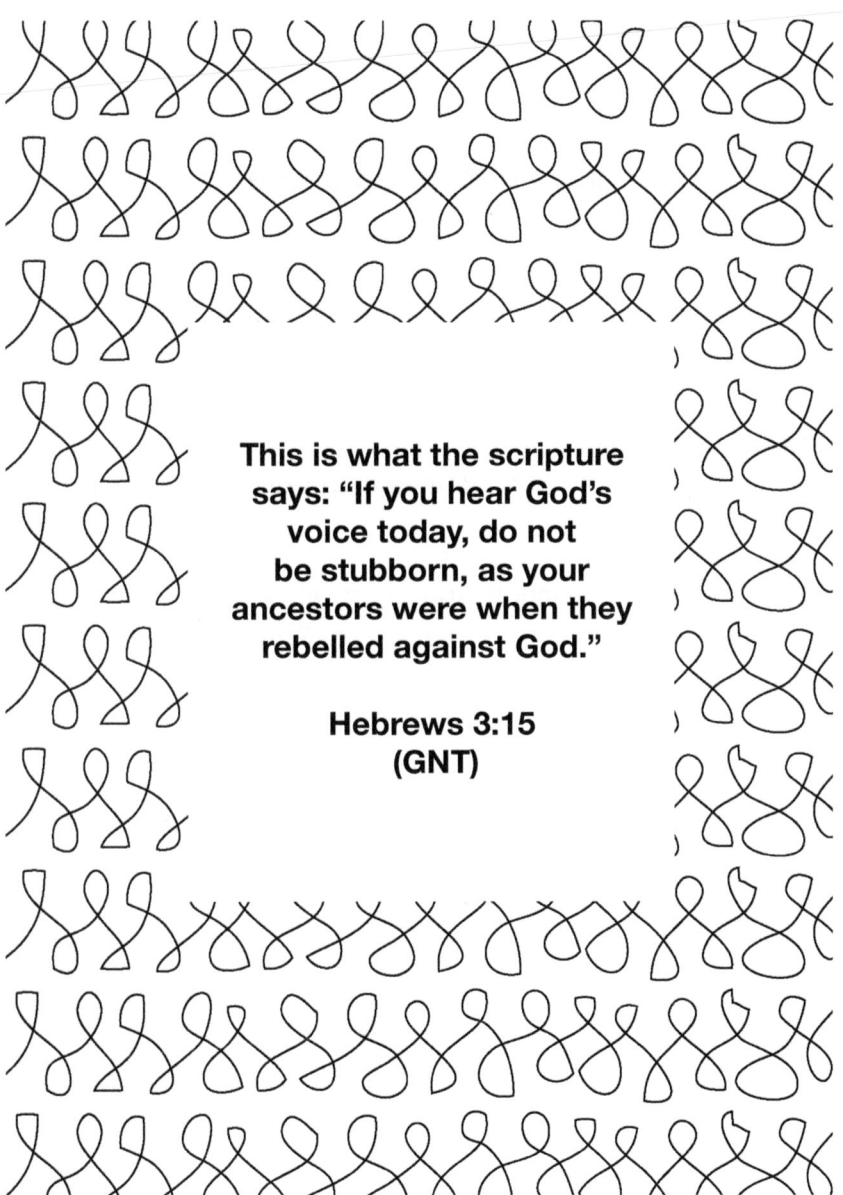

This is what the scripture says: "If you hear God's voice today, do not be stubborn, as your ancestors were when they rebelled against God."

Hebrews 3:15 (GNT)

#changedlandscape

I was driving along a road I hadn't been on for a while and noticed a new multi-storey car park. It looked nice, fit the spot and made the whole area look very different. Try as I may I couldn't recollect what was in the spot before. It made me think of how much more God can change things and give me hope for the situations I faced at the time.

God can change the landscape of any life such that we hardly remember what was before. Today, trust God for the change you desire.

Dear Father, thank you for the miraculous change the you effect in my life.

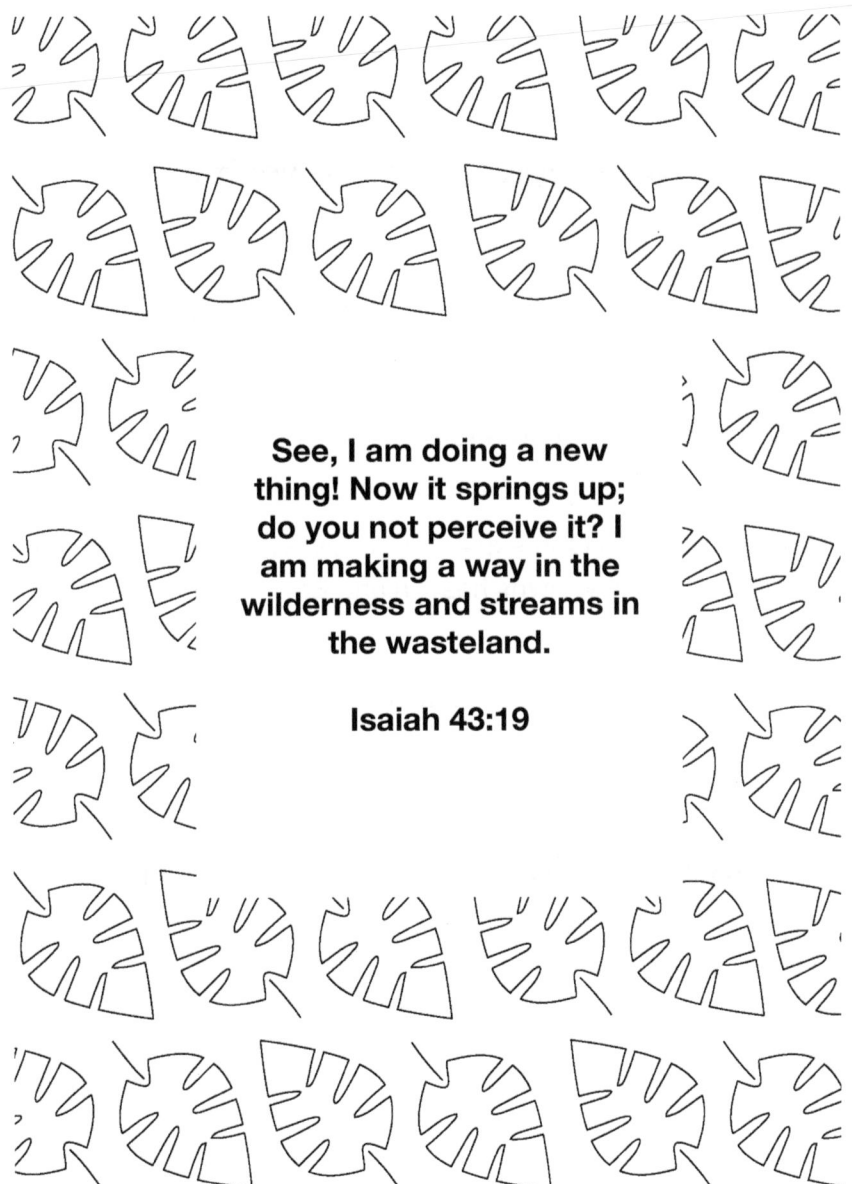

See, I am doing a new thing! Now it springs up; do you not perceive it? I am making a way in the wilderness and streams in the wasteland.

Isaiah 43:19

#whattogivehimwhoownsitall

It is less than three weeks to Christmas as I write this and naturally I am thinking of which gifts to give. In terms of what I can give God, all I have are things he has given me in the first place. Surely you can't wrap up and give someone the very gift they gave you?

However, that is all God expects from us. What perfect gift can we give the God who owns heaven and Earth? What he has first given us; ourselves.

So today, as every day, let us offer ourselves to God. That is the very best we can present.

Thank you, Father, for accepting the gift I offer.

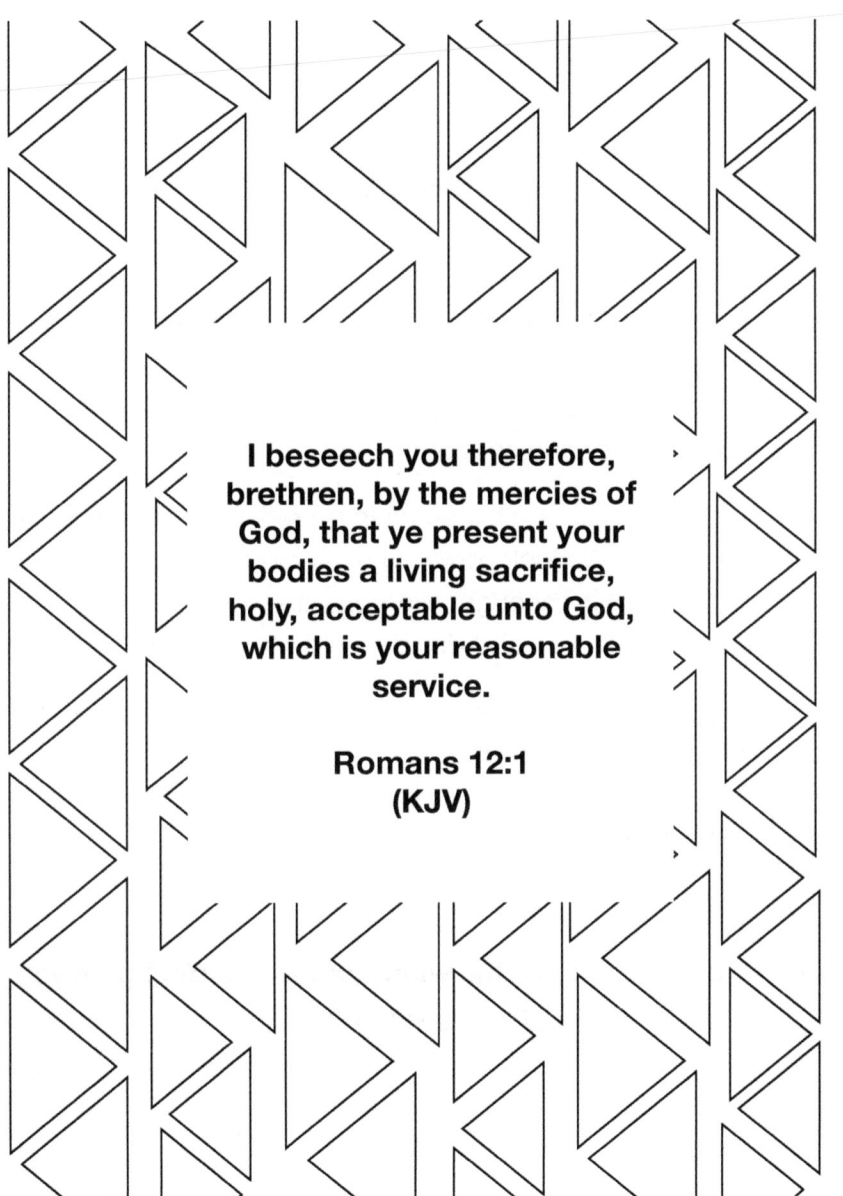

> I beseech you therefore, brethren, by the mercies of God, that ye present your bodies a living sacrifice, holy, acceptable unto God, which is your reasonable service.
>
> **Romans 12:1 (KJV)**

#untreasured

A few years ago, I bought my then four-year-old nephew a very trendy jumper as his Christmas present. We laugh about it now, but when he unwrapped the present and saw the jumper he threw it on the floor and spat out, "Rubbish!'

Sometimes, even as adults, we have no regard for the gifts we have been given. We look down on what God gives us, thinking it is not big or shiny enough. We compare what we have with what someone else has and decide we'd rather have their gift.

My nephew had to apologise and so do we. Forgive us Lord for those times we have not appreciated what you have given us. Please help us treasure the gifts you give us, knowing you give what is perfect for each one of us.

Thank you, Lord, for all the wonderful and perfect gifts you have given me.

Whatever is good and perfect comes down to us from God our Father.

James 1:17 (NLT)

#goingthroughthedark

I was driving home from visiting a client one dark winter evening when I got lost. I ended up in a very foggy patch along a back road but couldn't see the road ahead! Honestly, I was scared but I kept telling myself, "You may need to drive slowly but remember, there is a road and if you keep going you'll get home."

Sometimes, we go through a patch in life where we are scared and wonder if we will get through. It may be dark, and you may not be able to see your way through, but God's word says, "Do not be afraid, I am with you."[10] Whatever you face today, you can be assured of his presence with you.

Father, thank you that I don't need to fear because you are always near.

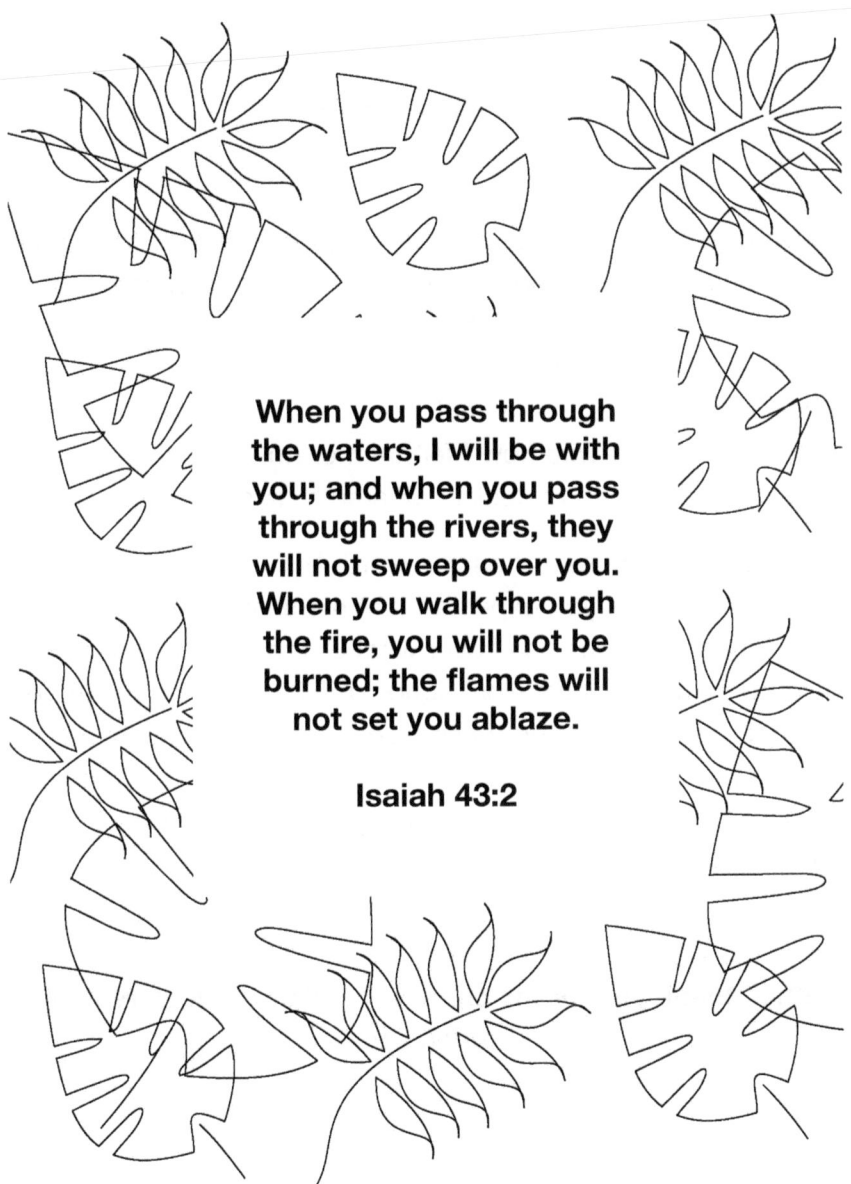

When you pass through the waters, I will be with you; and when you pass through the rivers, they will not sweep over you. When you walk through the fire, you will not be burned; the flames will not set you ablaze.

Isaiah 43:2

#getthememo

I have been to conferences where the presence of God was all so tangible, and I sensed my life about to take flight into a new dimension. Then, by the next week, I felt that I'm exactly where I was before the awesome atmosphere of the conference. In those times, I need to get the memo! The new season God promised had nothing to do with how I felt then or now. Things may look the same, but I need to declare differently; it is a new day!

Like me, you may have heard a word, but your reality doesn't match the change you expected. Let me share with you what I do in those situations: read over what God has said, change my thinking to match God's word, ignore my feelings and the temptation to describe my current situation, but start and continue to declare the change I expect. Let me encourage you, it may not feel like it just yet but in due season all will be as God said it will be.

Father, thank you for my change. I believe it, declare it and receive it.

For no word from God will ever fail

Luke 1:37

#rightallthewaythrough

Have you ever selected a lovely looking fruit and then cut through only to find it rotten inside? Just because it looks right on the outside doesn't mean it is right all the way to the core. In life, sometimes things just aren't really as they initially appear.

With that in mind, you may wonder how one can make the right choice. Thankfully, God has promised to help us make the right choice always. So, rather than just relying on what we know, we can trust him to lead us to what is right the whole way through.

Thank you, Father, for guiding me to make the right choices always.

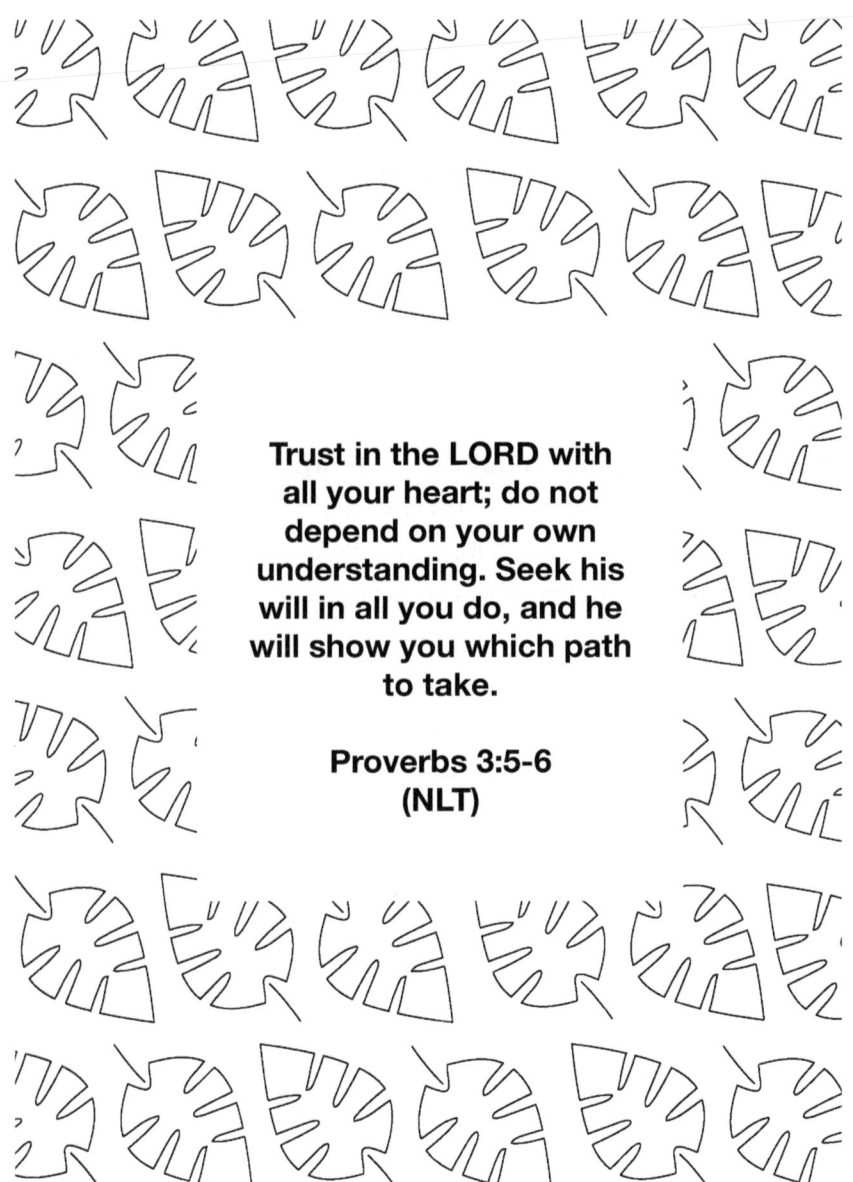

Trust in the LORD with all your heart; do not depend on your own understanding. Seek his will in all you do, and he will show you which path to take.

Proverbs 3:5-6 (NLT)

#wieldwithcare

In my home, every now and again someone needs reminding to be careful about the way they are holding or using a sharp knife.

Isaiah 49:2 likens our mouth to a sharpened sword. People don't generally go about playing with a sharp knife or sword but handle it with care. In like manner, as we go about our day, let us ensure we wield the sword of our mouth with care.

Thank you, Lord, for your help in using my tongue to please you always.

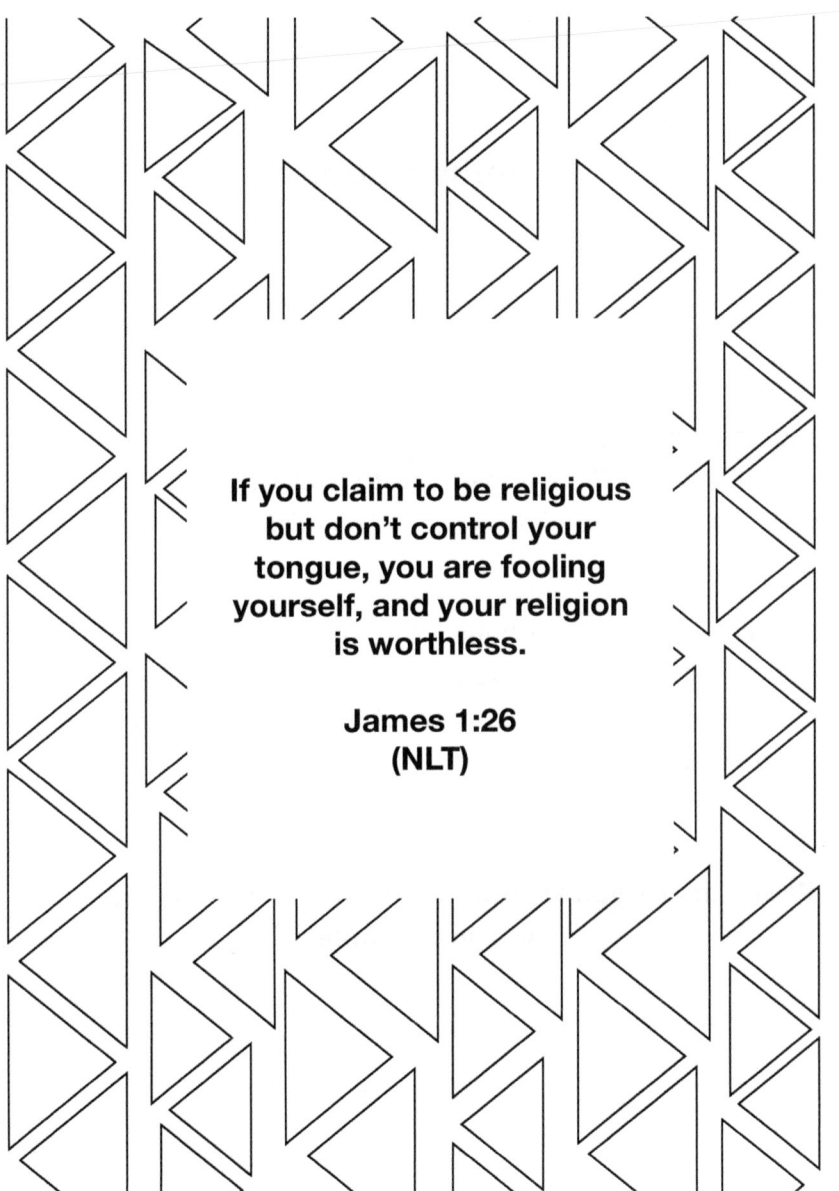

If you claim to be religious but don't control your tongue, you are fooling yourself, and your religion is worthless.

James 1:26 (NLT)

#togetherstronger

Some of us are better at building relationships than others. Though sometimes they can be difficult, we all know that we are better in relationship with others than not. However, if you ever doubted it, the Bible story in Judges 18 should be a warning. Verse 28 states, *"There was no one to rescue them because they lived a long way from Sidon and had no relationship with anyone else."*

How awful to be in trouble and have no one to call on! Relationships can be started in so many ways, however, they very rarely grow and remain without effort. Be intentional today; build relationship.

Father, thank you for putting me in relationship with you and your people.

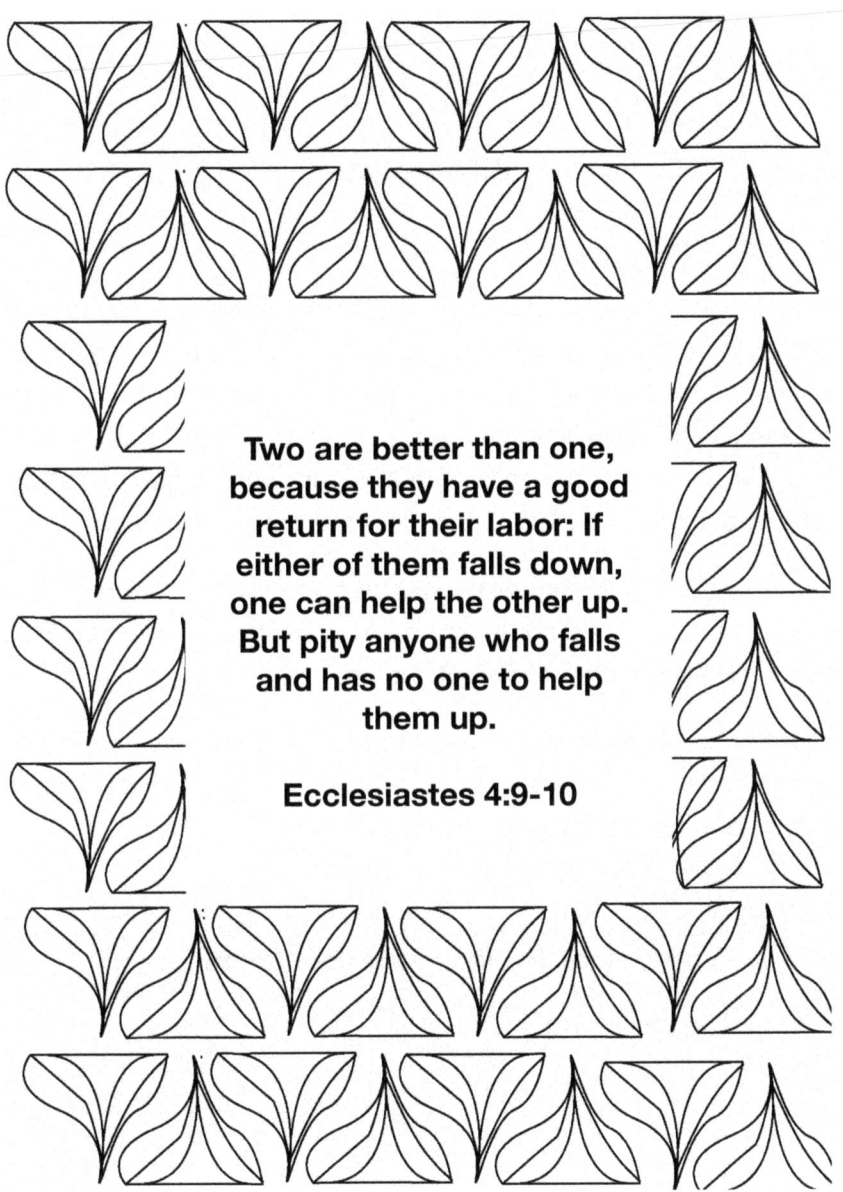

Two are better than one, because they have a good return for their labor: If either of them falls down, one can help the other up. But pity anyone who falls and has no one to help them up.

Ecclesiastes 4:9-10

#itsnotfair

I heard this lady talk about her heightened sense of justice and dislike for unfairness. I understood what she meant, however, justice is not the same as fairness. Fairness is that everyone gets equal, but that may not be just. Imagine one of those all-inclusive children's choirs; giving everyone a solo part might be fair but definitely not just to the kid who really can't sing!

As a mum, I remember, when my girls were younger, trying my best to sort out one dispute or the other. Despite my best efforts, invariably someone will cry out, "It's not fair!"

Thankfully, the Bible never says God is fair, but it does say he is just. Whatever the situation we face, we can trust him to do what is right and best for each one of us always.

Dear Father, thank you for your faithfulness to me always.

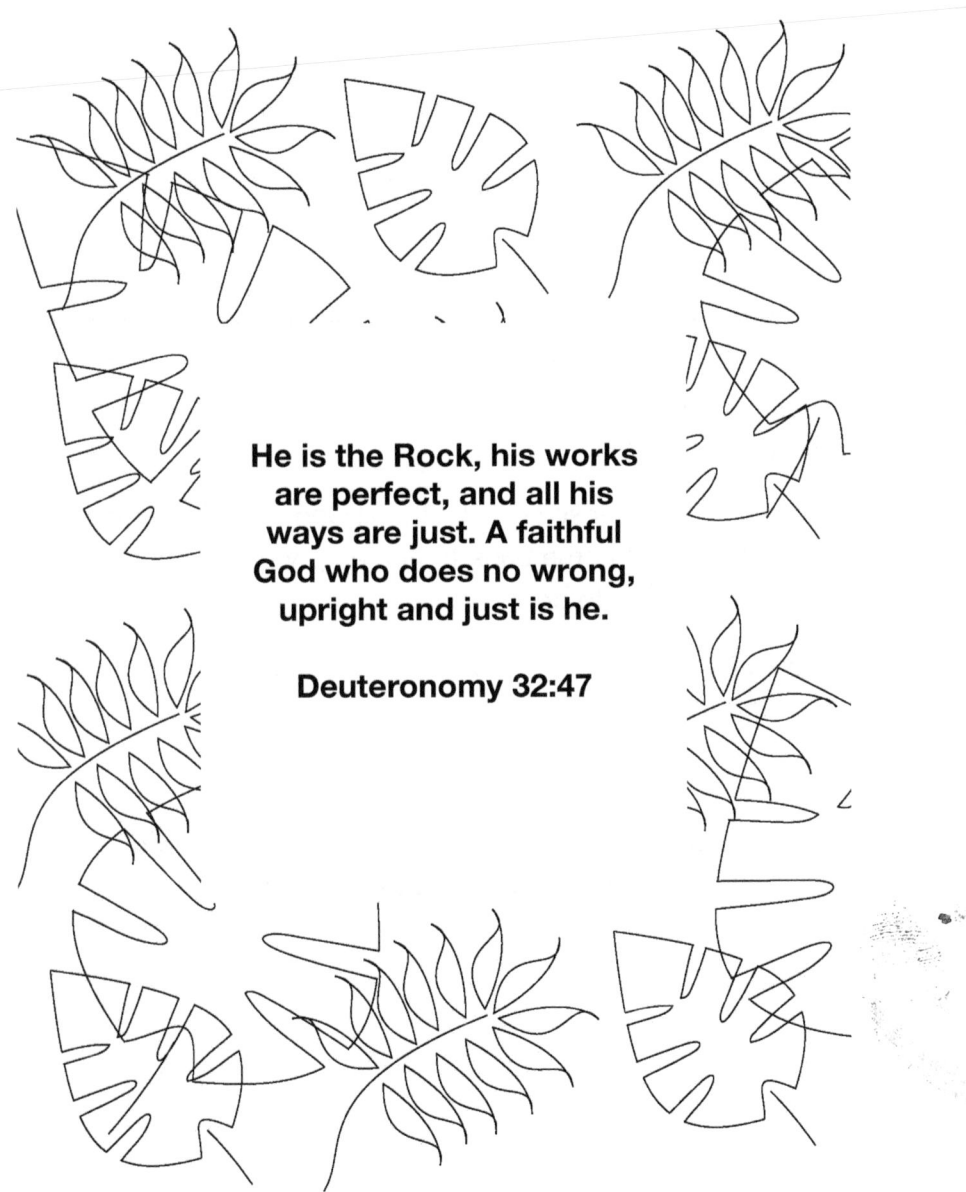

He is the Rock, his works are perfect, and all his ways are just. A faithful God who does no wrong, upright and just is he.

Deuteronomy 32:47

#echo

It is always fun watching a child experience an echo. They find it amusing to hear their own words come back to them. God, the Father, takes delight in hearing his words come back to him through his children.

We are to echo, ever so confidently, all God says; for he has said his words will not come back to him empty but will accomplish what he sent them to do [11].

Whatever you are going through today, choose to boldly echo what God has said about you and your situation.

**Thank you, Father, for the confidence to echo
all you have said about me.**

For He Himself has said, "I will never leave you nor forsake you." So we may boldly say: "The Lord is my helper;
I will not fear.

Hebrews 13:5-6 (NKJV)

#loveprepared

I was ready for a fight. I had played out the conversation in my head and got all my responses ready to fire. However, somewhere in the middle of the conversation, I realised that despite my antagonistic attitude, the person who was supposed to be in the fight with me wasn't at all up for it. How much nicer the whole situation would have been if I had prepared to be nice!

Even before we did anything, God decided that his attitude towards us would be love. Ephesians 1:5 (GW) states, *'Because of his love he had already decided to adopt us through Jesus Christ. He freely chose to do this.'*

Seeing as we have received God's love, let us be prepared to give the same. Today, determine beforehand to love.

Thank you, Father, for deciding ahead to love me and for helping me decide to have a loving attitude today.

This is my commandment: Love each other in the same way I have loved you.

John 15:12
(NLT)

#thebodyguard

It is the night before a major event. Bound with chains between two soldiers and about to be executed the next morning, Peter, as we read in Acts 12, is asleep! That is the kind of peace the Bible describes as surpassing all comprehension which will guard our hearts and minds in Christ Jesus (see Philippians 4:7).

Looking up the word 'guard', it means to keep watch like a military sentinel, taking any defensive and offensive means necessary. God's peace has been assigned to guard our hearts and minds as we trust him to do so. Therefore, we can each rest in the knowledge that we are well protected.

Father, thank you for your peace that guards me always.

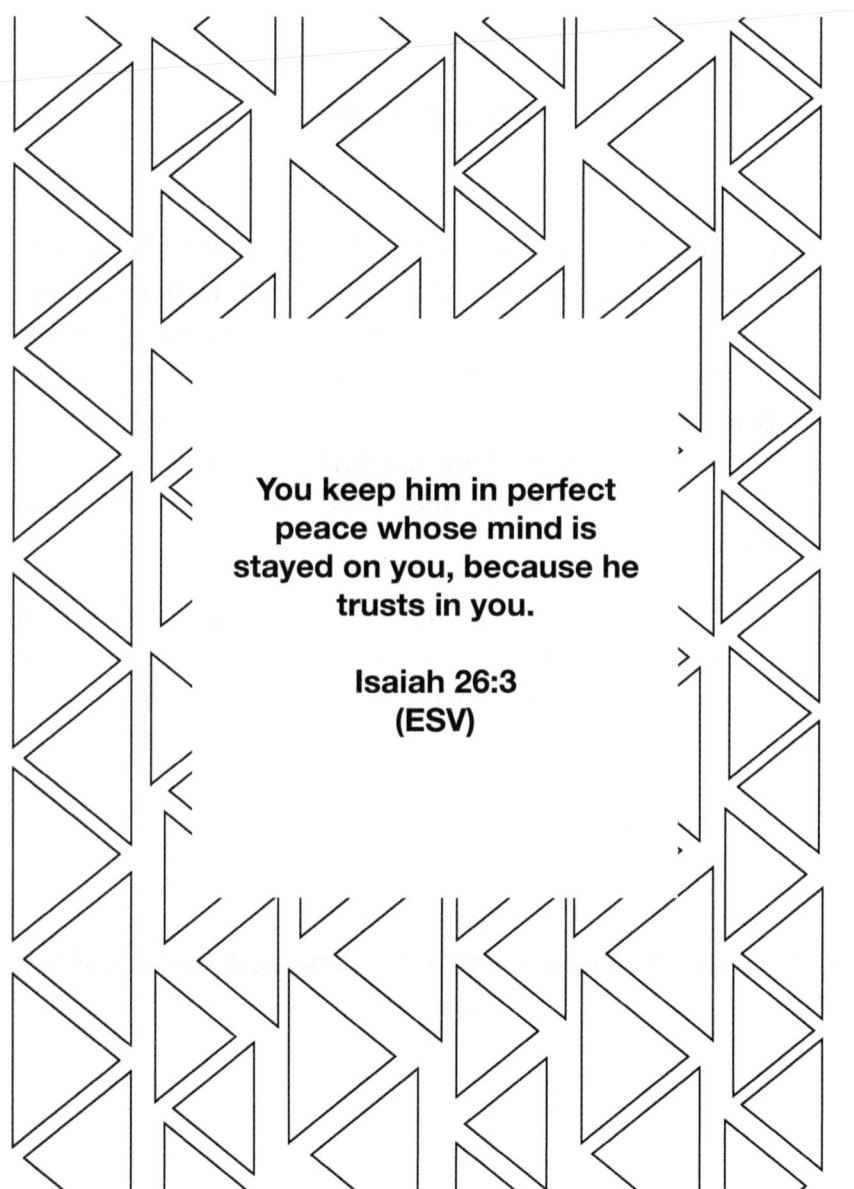

You keep him in perfect peace whose mind is stayed on you, because he trusts in you.

**Isaiah 26:3
(ESV)**

#daddyknows

When my children were younger and needed something, they simply asked and expected it to be provided. They didn't bother themselves with whether their dad or mum had money or plans for any money they might have. As far they were concerned, their parents were there to meet whatever need they had. Of course, we taught them they couldn't have everything they wanted but we did provide for their needs, like any parent would be expected to.

Well, guess what, we have a Father who has promised to meet our needs. Even better, he is fully able to provide all we could ever need, and it is his pleasure to do so. Luke 12:32 (KJV) states, *"Fear not, little flock; for it is your Father's good pleasure to give you the kingdom."* So, do not be afraid because you have a need, simply talk to your Heavenly Father about it.

Thank you, Father, for being willing and able to meet all my needs.

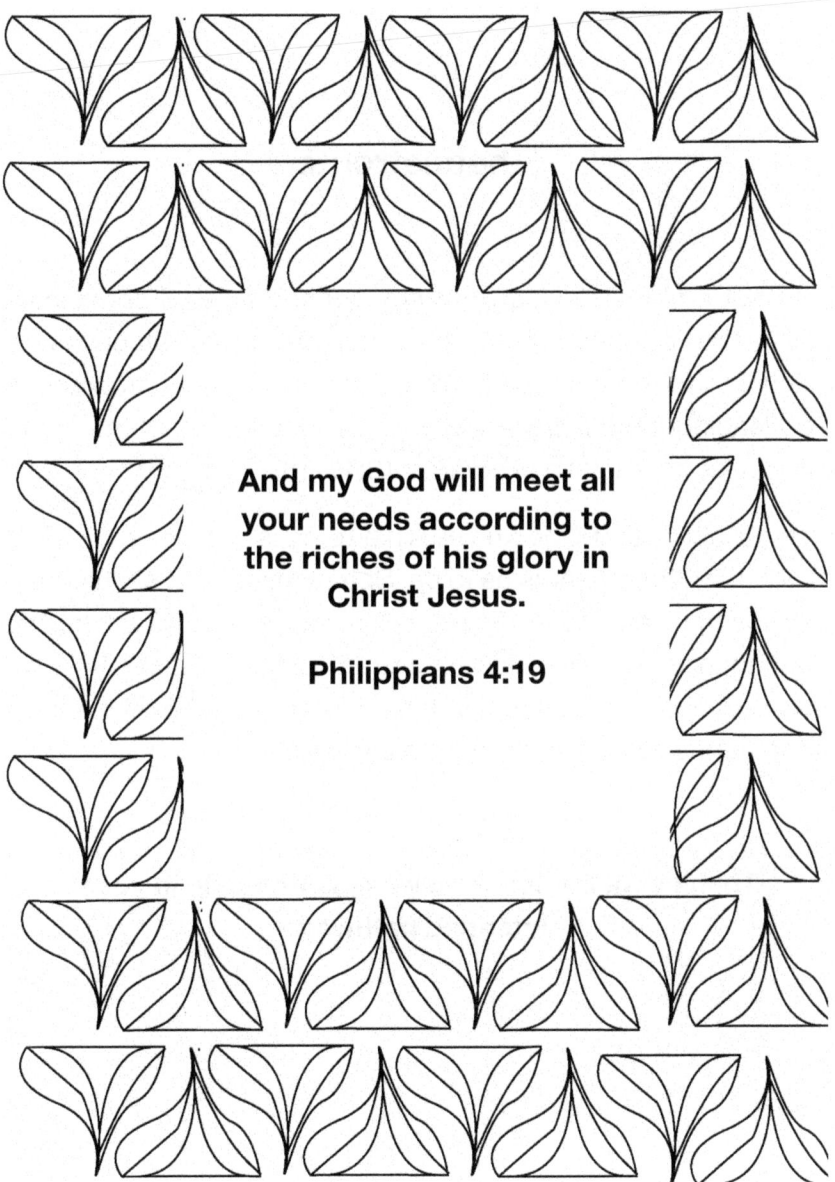

And my God will meet all your needs according to the riches of his glory in Christ Jesus.

Philippians 4:19

#thebestroute

I am not a fan of driving on windy country lanes. I sometimes opt to take a longer, more straightforward route rather than a much shorter country road. With that in mind, I can appreciate God leading the children of Israel on a longer route through the wilderness as we read in Exodus 13:17-18.

I am delighted that God knows what route is best for each of us to get to where he wants us to be. Sometimes, we wish the route was different and other times, we think we should be further along than we are. Regardless of what we think about where we are in our lives, we can rest in the knowledge that God leads us in the right way and at the right pace always.

Thank you, Father, for always guiding me in your intended pathway.

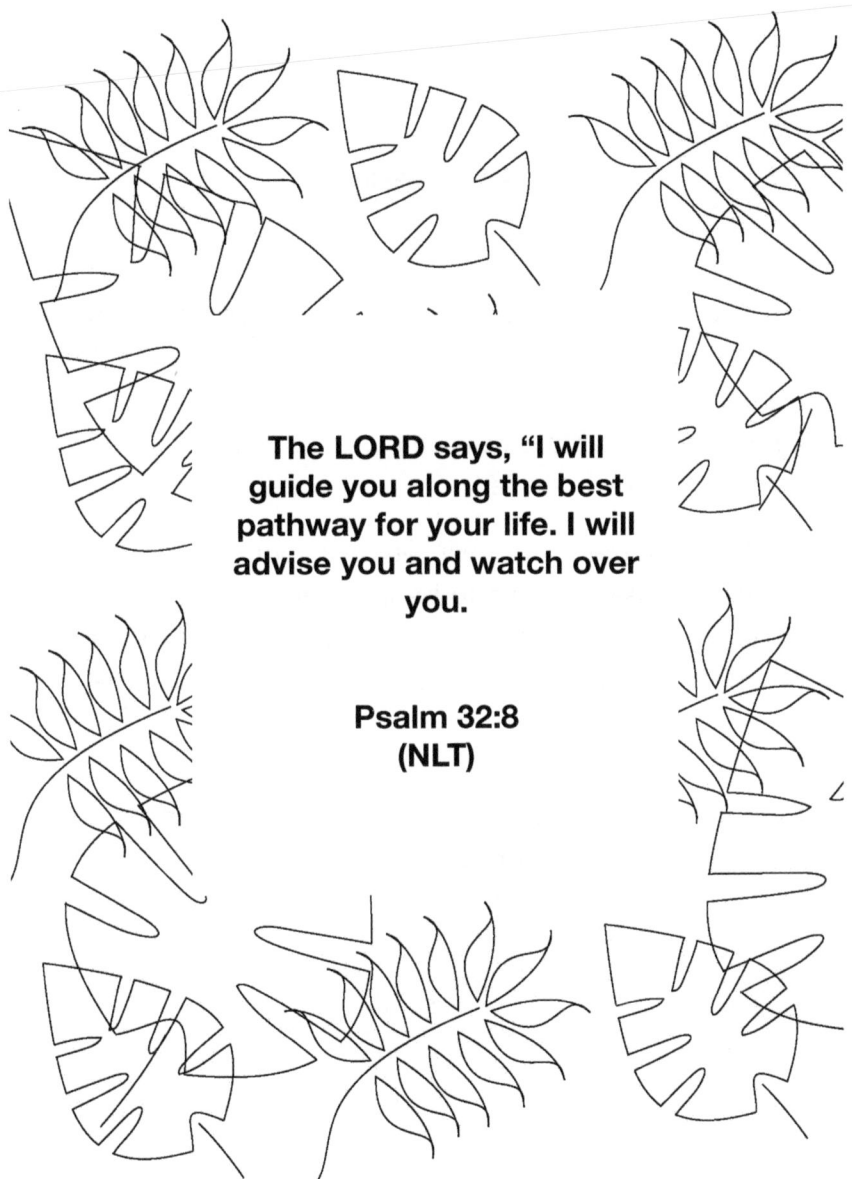

The LORD says, "I will guide you along the best pathway for your life. I will advise you and watch over you.

Psalm 32:8
(NLT)

#justserve

I write this the day after Andy Murray won Wimbledon for the second time, so I thought I'd get tennis in somewhat. Most of us want to win. We want to do well and rise to the top wherever God has placed us. Usually, we think this comes by striving and focusing on our own hustle.

In the New Testament, however, we read about James and John and how they asked Jesus to be in the top spot. Interestingly, when Jesus showed them how, it was not as they expected. He taught them that to win in life, as in tennis, we must serve.

Dear Jesus, thank you for the example you set for me; being Lord of all yet serving.

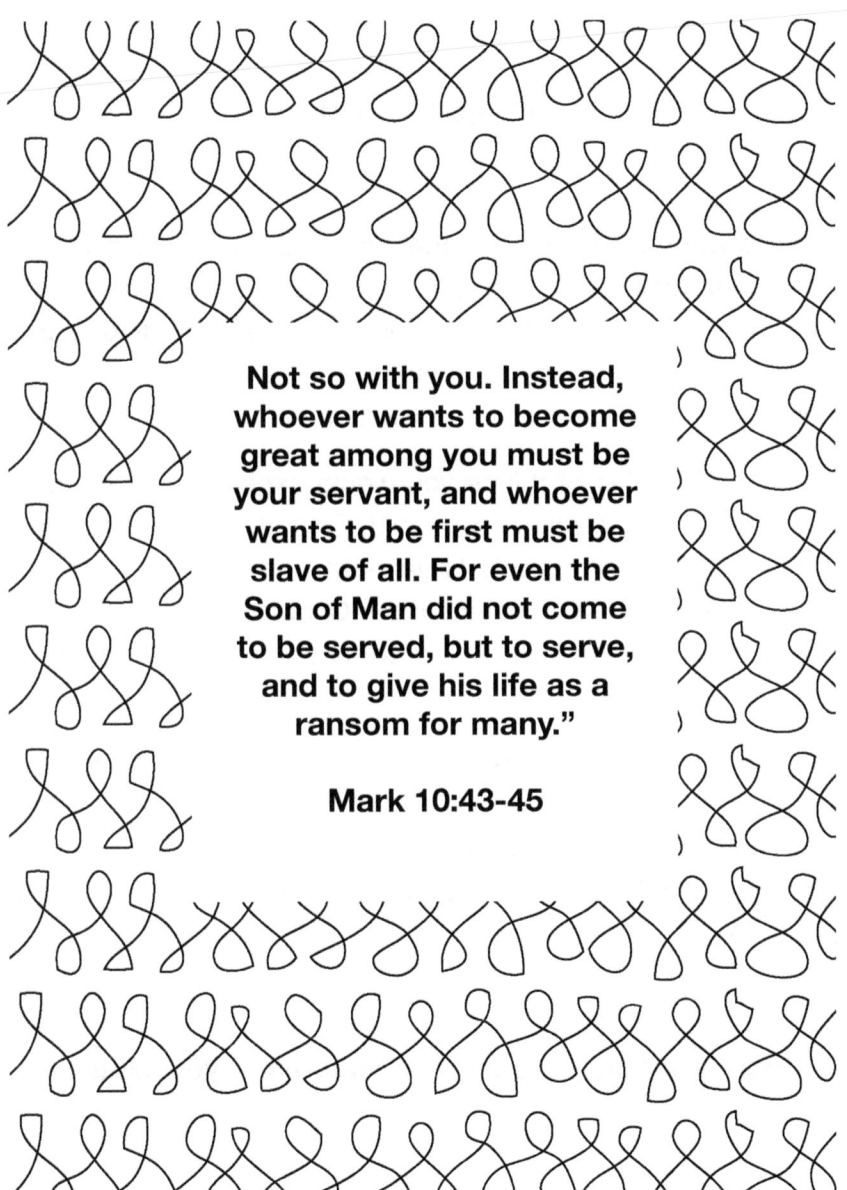

Not so with you. Instead, whoever wants to become great among you must be your servant, and whoever wants to be first must be slave of all. For even the Son of Man did not come to be served, but to serve, and to give his life as a ransom for many."

Mark 10:43-45

#allgrownup

When newborns cry, they get attention. They can't talk, and crying is their means of communication. As that baby begins to grow, the parents learn that not every cry needs attending to and the child also learns to communicate in other ways. In effect, there is a gradual process of growing up.

There is a long list of things you would expect of a baby that you would not of a school age child. Or that you would expect of a teenager but not of a thirty-year-old. The same is true in our spirit life. The more we mature in our Christian life the more we should do away with childish behaviour and exhibit the character of a grown up.

The Bible, in 1 Corinthians 13:11 reads, *"When I was a child, I spoke as a child, I understood as a child, I thought as a child; but when I became a man, I put away childish things."* The question today is, does my maturity show in the way I speak, understand and think?

Dear Father, help me to be as matured as you expect.

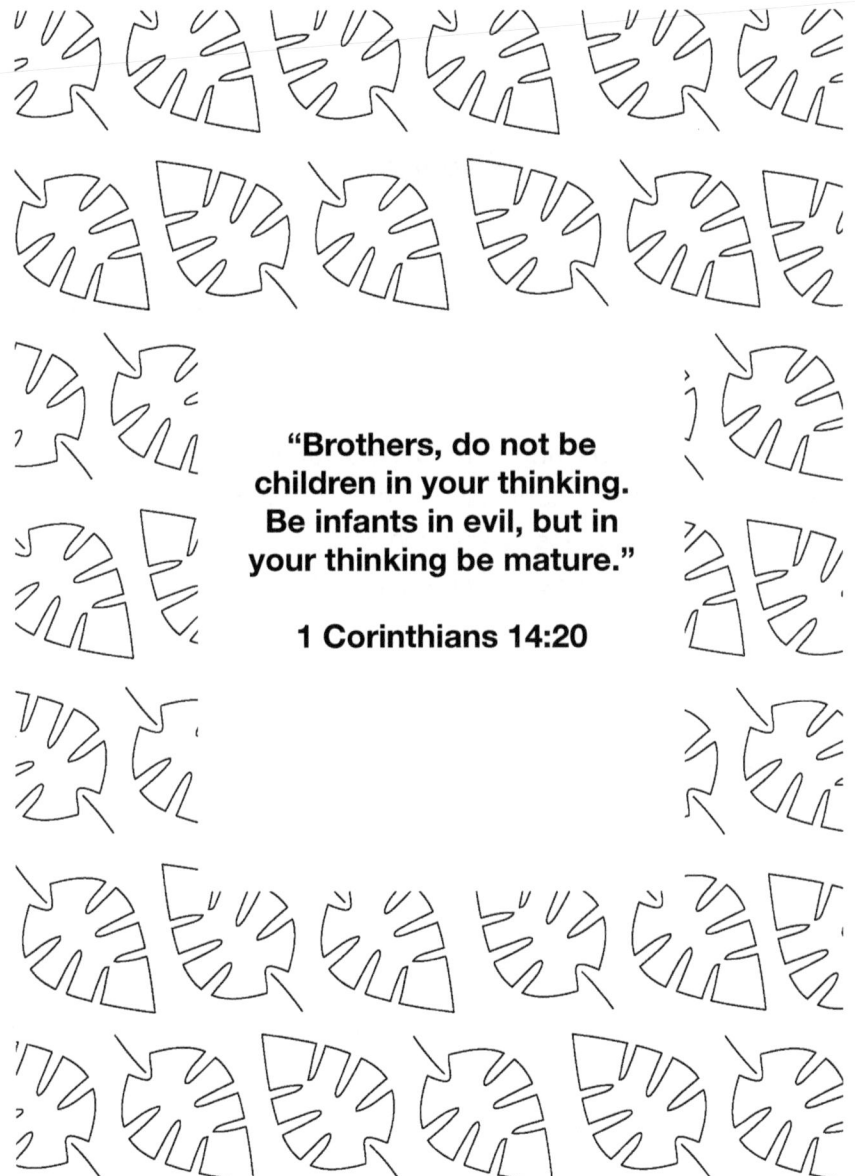

"Brothers, do not be children in your thinking. Be infants in evil, but in your thinking be mature."

1 Corinthians 14:20

#delight

I have met people who view God as an oppressive ruler, intent on judging people who neglect his rules. But this is not the true heart of God.

The Bible makes us understand God takes great pleasure in being merciful. You might have known a harsh parent, a strict teacher or plain old mean person in your life but rejoice today in the knowledge your Heavenly Father's great delight is to be kind towards you.

Thank you, Father, for your great love and kindness towards me.

Who is a God like you, who pardons sin and forgives the transgression of the remnant of his inheritance? You do not stay angry forever but delight to show mercy.

Micah 7:18

#sleephappy

As I sit writing this at half past mid-night, my mind has turned towards my bed and sleep. I have seen enough TV programmes and heard first hand from people who suffer from lack of sleep to know that having a good night's sleep is not anything to be taken for granted. I am glad that our Heavenly Father grants sleep to those he loves [12]. So tonight, sleep happy in the promise of God.

For every good night's sleep you have granted me, Lord, I'm thankful.

When I lie down, I go to sleep in peace; you alone, O Lord, keep me perfectly safe.

Psalm 4:8 (GNT)

#beyondthepaygrade

In 2 Chronicles 24:2 we read that Jehoiada was a priest and yet further on in the chapter, in verse 16, we read that he was buried with the kings because of the good he had done in Israel. The recount of Jehoiada's life makes us realise we don't need to hold a position or have a title to be effective in what God has called us to do and receive the reward of being faithful.

Maybe at work you are left with tasks beyond your pay grade, maybe at home you are doing it all without support. In whatever situation you are expected to do more than should be required, let me encourage you, do it as unto God. With or without a title, with or without due recognition, like Jehoiada, where you are faithful, God will ensure you are rewarded.

Thank you, Lord, that I can trust you for a just reward.

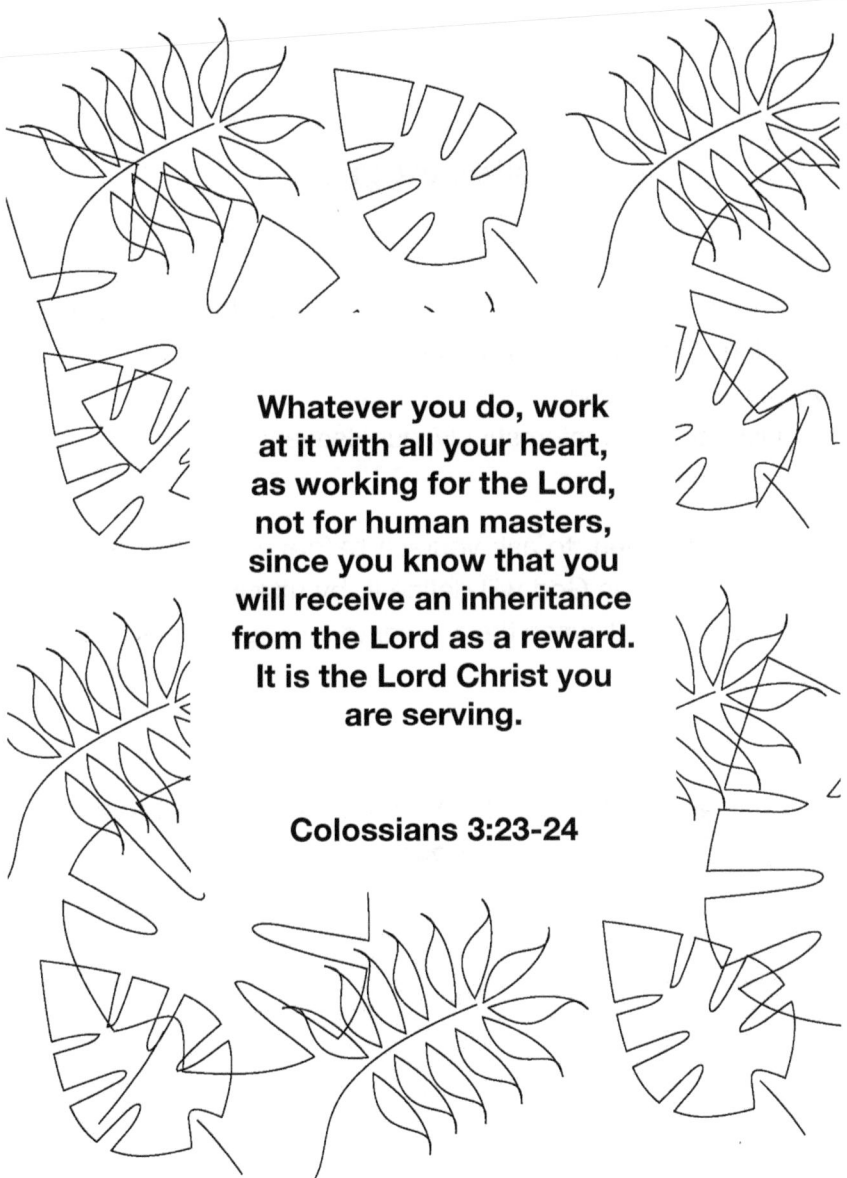

Whatever you do, work at it with all your heart, as working for the Lord, not for human masters, since you know that you will receive an inheritance from the Lord as a reward. It is the Lord Christ you are serving.

Colossians 3:23-24

#talkinggift

Any parent will tell you, those singing and talking toys soon get annoying. My sister-in-law once gave my daughter a present, a five-piece musical set! I looked at it and thought, that is going to be 'missing' soon. Interestingly, our Heavenly Father does want us to give talking gifts.

The question, then, to ask yourself before you speak is, 'Will I be giving a gift, as God will define it, by uttering what is on my mind?' Only speak when the answer to that question is a definite yes.

Thank you, Father, for helping me speak words that do good.

Watch the way you talk. Let nothing foul or dirty come out if your mouth. Say only what helps, each word a gift.

Ephesians 4:29 (MSG)

#ridiculousmiracle

The ridiculous nature of many miracles in the Bible never ceases to amaze me. For example, how does a slingshot and a small stone kill a giant and make him fall face down? Or how does water turn into the best wine served at a wedding party?

One of the key things we see in these miracles is how the people involved did what they could regardless of how ridiculous it was. At the wedding in Cana, Mary wisely warned the servants, "Do whatever he asks you to do." If not, I can imagine one of them might have said to Jesus, "It's wine that is needed not water" and with that ignored his request for the water pots to be filled.

What is it that you are praying about and what has God told you to do? Does it seem ridiculous in the light of what you need? For example, do you need healing but sense God asking you to forgive someone who has hurt you? Or do you need some food but sense God asking you to make a meal for someone else? All I can advise is an echo of Mary's words; do whatever God has told you to do.

If you will obey and do the seemingly ridiculous you will see the miraculous.

Thank you, Jesus, for helping me obey you.

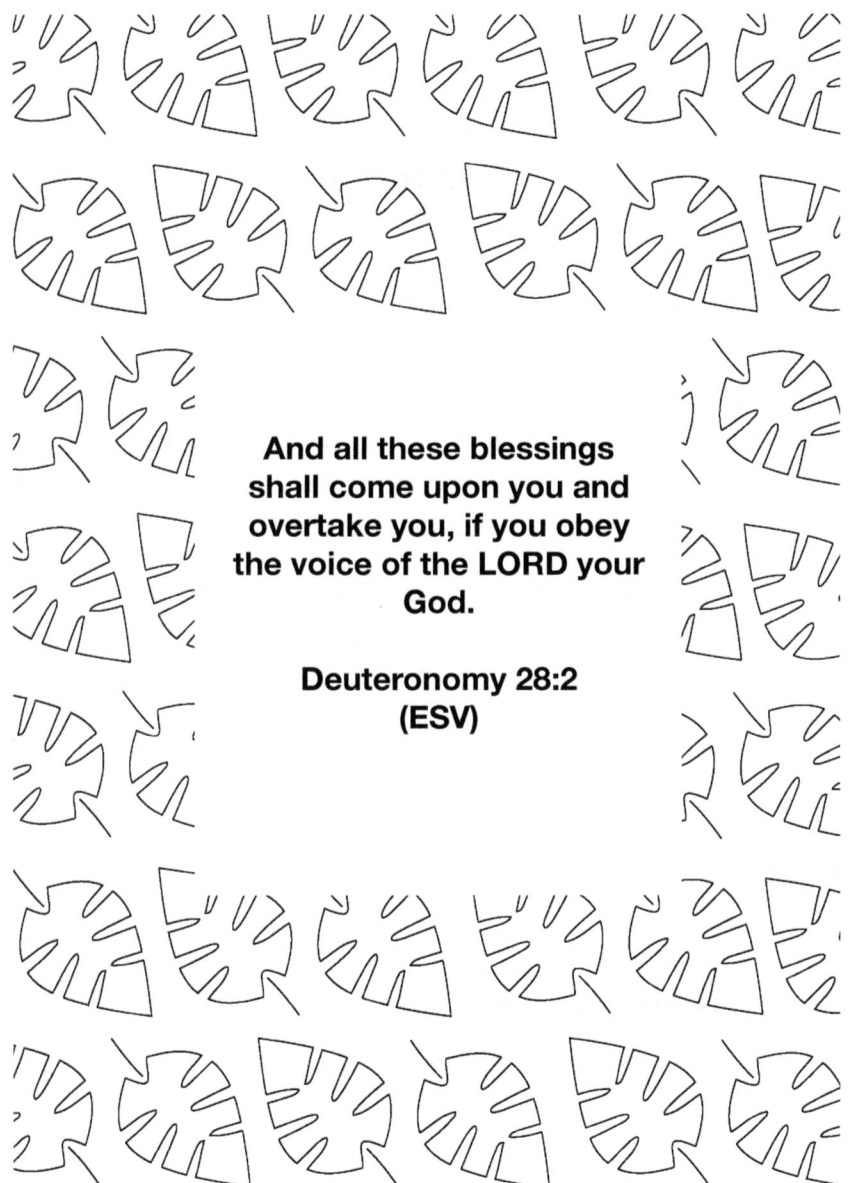

And all these blessings shall come upon you and overtake you, if you obey the voice of the LORD your God.

Deuteronomy 28:2 (ESV)

#thetodolist

My colleague once told me how, as a young boy, whenever his dad asked him to take a glass of water to someone, he'll add, "Look where you are going and take the water with you." I thought that was a wise thing to say as most times when the admonition to a child is, "Don't spill the water," they get so focused on not spilling the water they end up doing exactly that.

Wisdom teaches us to focus on the things we should be doing. When we do that, we'll find we do less of the things we shouldn't do. For instance, if you focus on loving people you'll find you are not impatient with them, you don't judge them, and you don't gossip about them.

Let's each decide today to follow wisdom and focus on the 'to do' list.

Dear Father, thank you for helping me set my focus right.

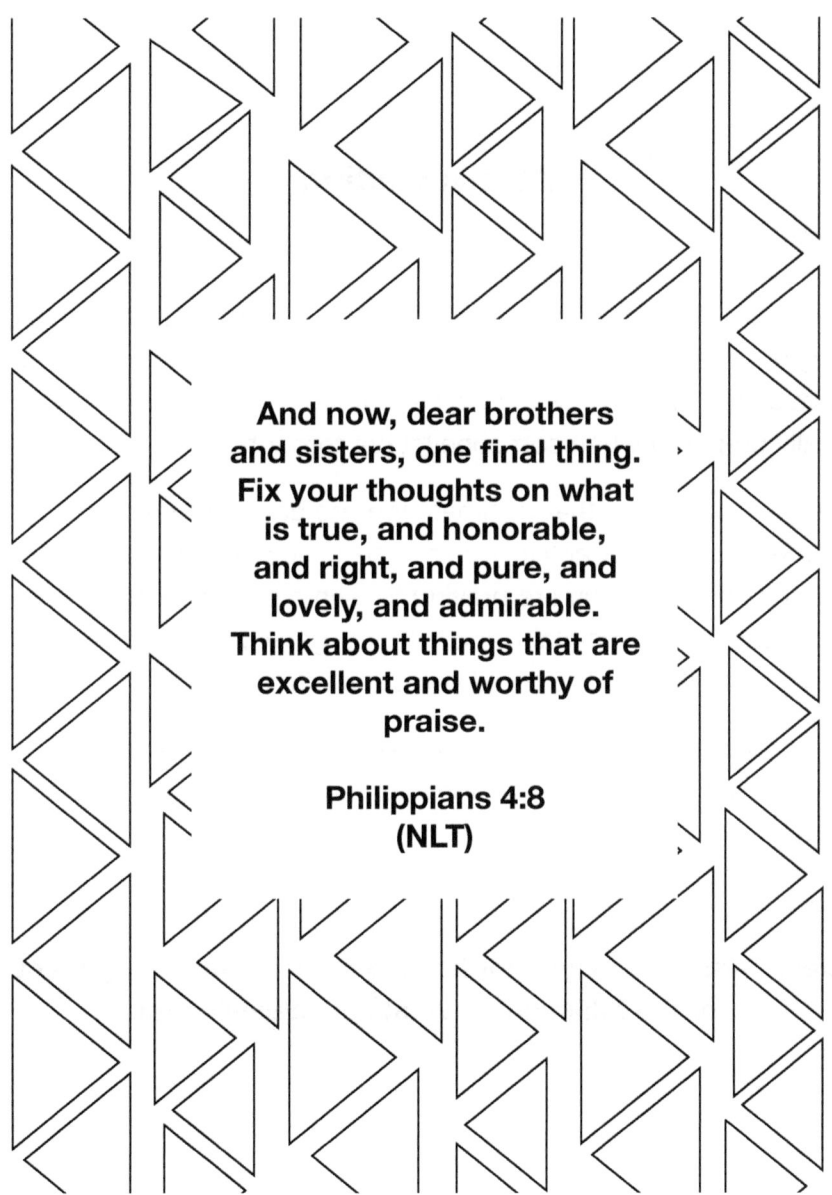

And now, dear brothers and sisters, one final thing. Fix your thoughts on what is true, and honorable, and right, and pure, and lovely, and admirable. Think about things that are excellent and worthy of praise.

Philippians 4:8 (NLT)

#activewaiting

I signalled for her to go yet she didn't move. In fact, she wasn't paying attention and so missed a chance. It amused me that though the lady was waiting in her car at the junction she wasn't really prepared when someone let her through.

We all can be like that at times. We are actively praying about something but not actively doing the things we can to prepare for the answer. If you are praying to own a car, for instance, are you learning to maintain one? If God gave you the thing you have been praying for, could you cope with it?

Waiting is not passive. Yes, it involves being patient and trusting God, but it also involves action. Get ready, the answer is on the way!

Dear Father, thank you for helping me to be actively patient for the fulfilment of what I am believing for.

But they that wait upon the Lord shall renew their strength; they shall mount up with wings as eagles; they shall run, and not be weary; and they shall walk, and not faint.

Isaiah 40:31

#cometodaddy

I was desperately holding back my tears. All I wanted to do was head to my bed. However, as I walked into the house, my dad, sat in his favourite seat, looked at me and immediately put down the newspaper he was reading. All he said was, "Come," motioning with his hands for me to sit on his lap. You might think I was five or something but no, I was an upset teenager.

It is a great comfort that no matter how old we are or what we are going through, God's loving arms are open wide towards us. The Father beckons each one of us to come to him for all we need today.

Thank you, Father, for your care and love in calling me to you, especially when the going seems tough.

Come to me, all you who are weary and burdened, and I will give you rest.

Matthew 11:28

#changechallenge

I have had a work laptop for a few years now and I can use it with ease. All was fine until the battery stopped charging and would only work when plugged into the mains. Thankfully, I got a new one. My new laptop has an upgraded software, so things don't work exactly like they did on my old one and I find myself opting to go back to the old laptop, despite its limited functionality.

That may be somewhat trivial, but you may identify with the scenario. Maybe you've wanted a change but now it has come you find yourself wishing for or actually going back to what was because the change brought more of a challenge than you were prepared for. Whatever the situation, it is not time to revert or wish you could. Instead it is time to trust God for help and dig deep. You can press on with his help and fully embrace the best that is to come.

Thank you, Father, for the strength and courage to follow through the change you bring my way.

He gives strength to those who are tired; to the ones who lack power, he gives renewed energy.

Isaiah 40:29
(NET)

#Lplates

Two of my daughters are currently learning to drive. The other day one of them asked me a question to do with driving and I really had to think about the answer. You see, when you start learning, each action is carefully considered. If you want to make a turn, for instance, you first think about looking through your mirrors, decelerating, declutching. Once you are well practised, however, you do all those things almost automatically.

It is a well-known fact that the more you do something, the easier it gets. This holds true in every area of our lives, including our spiritual growth. Initially, we have to remember to read our Bible, pray, show love, watch what we say etc., but as we continue doing these things they become habits.

Be determined, whatever stage you are at, to keep up the practice of godliness, so it becomes your nature and your life.

Thank you, Lord Jesus, for helping me practice godliness and be more like you every day.

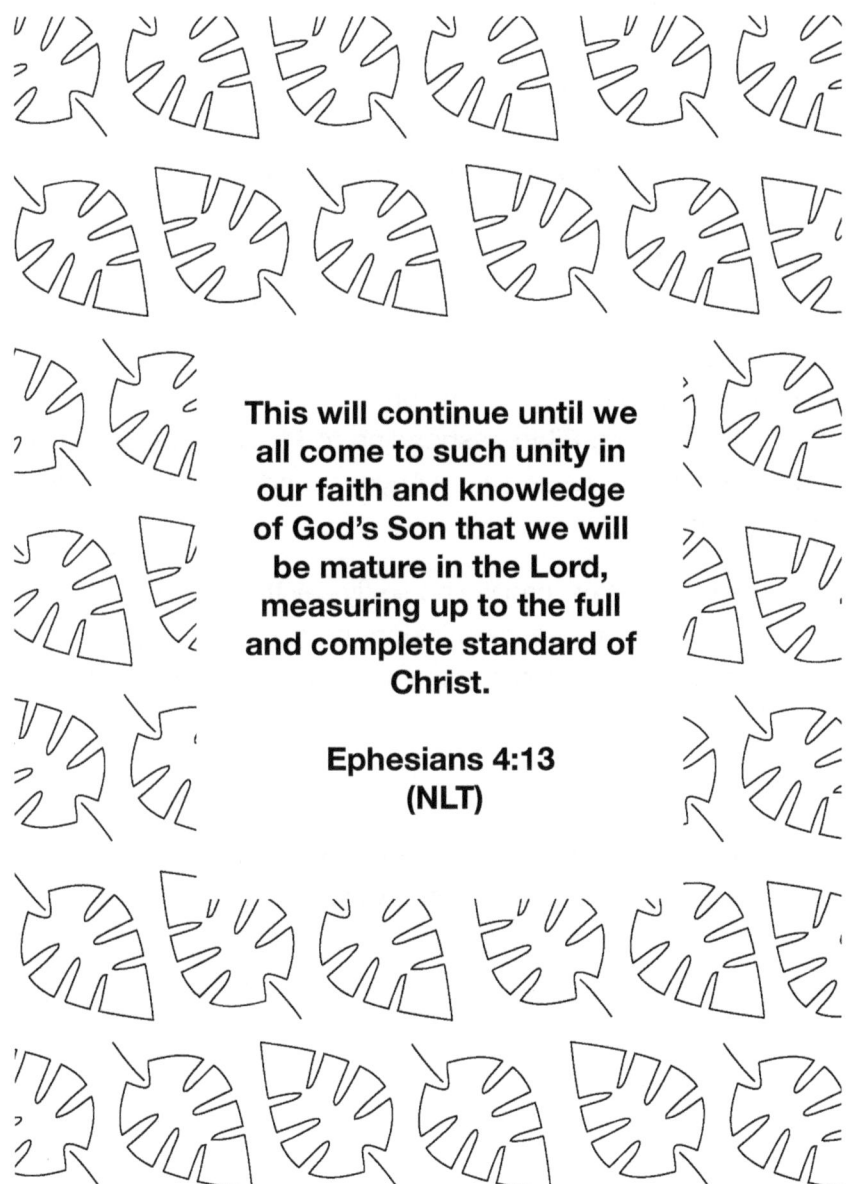

This will continue until we all come to such unity in our faith and knowledge of God's Son that we will be mature in the Lord, measuring up to the full and complete standard of Christ.

Ephesians 4:13 (NLT)

#closeresemblance

A friend reminded me the other day that she had never met my oldest daughter. Thinking about this afterwards, I couldn't help but think she kind of has. My daughter looks very much like me, only younger. In the Bible, responding to Phillip's request to be shown the Father, Jesus said, "Anyone who has seen me has seen the Father [13]."

When people meet us, can we honestly say they have met God? Do they leave our presence thinking the same? Today, like the title of a hymn I remember singing as a youngster, let others see Jesus in you.

Dear Father, thank you for helping me reflect you more each day.

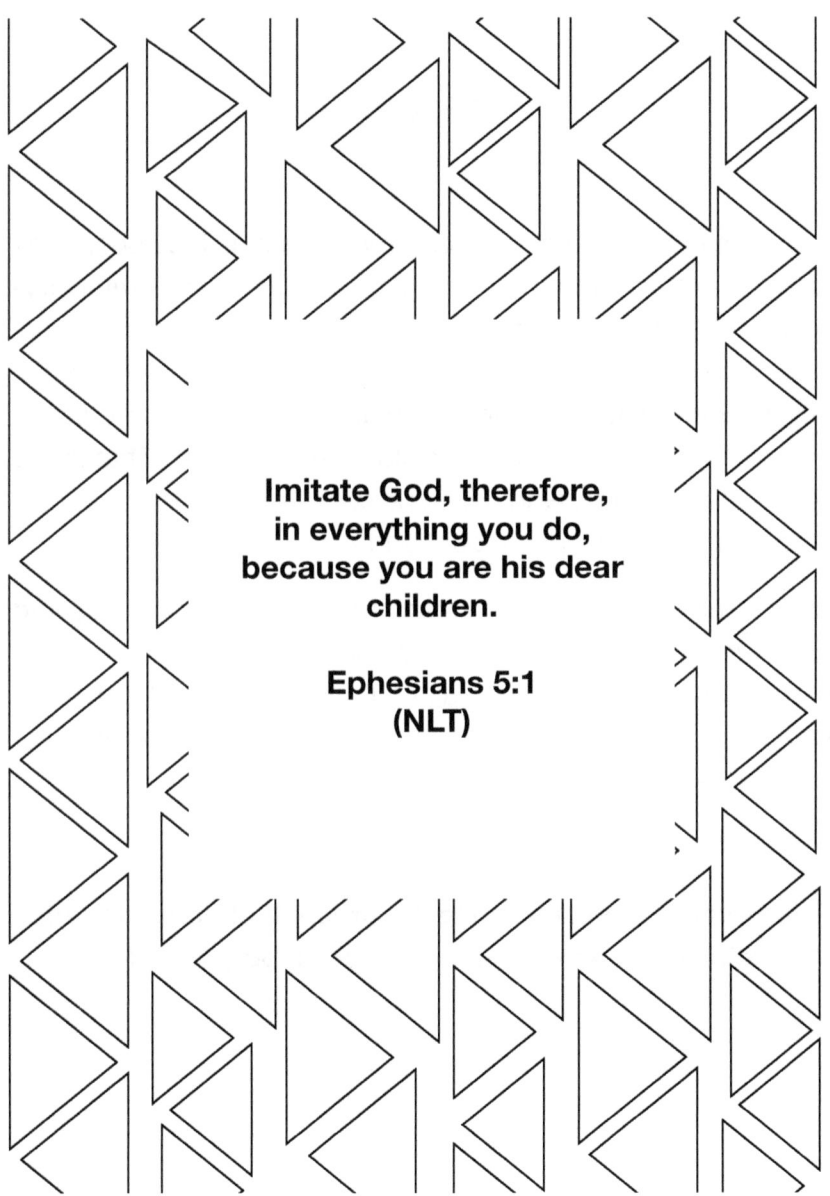

Imitate God, therefore, in everything you do, because you are his dear children.

Ephesians 5:1
(NLT)

#goyou

Imagine a parent about to enter a room. Just as they peep their head through the door they notice their toddler desperately trying to reach a toy, far back on the settee. The parent stops, wanting to see if the child will manage to get the toy. Of course, they want the child to, though silent and watching intently, inside they are shouting, "Go on my child, you can do it!" That is the picture of our Father, God, when he sees us reaching out in faith for the things he has put in our hearts.

I don't know what you are reaching out for, but be assured God is rooting for you, his eyes are watching over you and his good pleasure is to give you all you could ever need [14]. Let me encourage you to be strong and courageous. Do not be afraid or discouraged for the Lord, your God, is with you.

Thank you, Father, for being my greatest cheerleader and for helping me achieve everything you purposed for me.

So do not fear, for I am with you; do not be dismayed, for I am your God. I will strengthen you and help you; I will uphold you with my righteous right hand.

Isaiah 41:10

APPENDIX 1

How to invite Jesus Christ into your life as Saviour and Lord

To become a Christian is to have personal relationship with Jesus Christ. God, because of his great love for us, has made it simple for us to have that relationship. What is required is that we each believe in Jesus Christ as our Saviour, ask him to forgive our sin, and to be our Lord.

There are no specific words that must be used to ask Jesus into our lives as Saviour and Lord, but you could speak to God using the following prayer as a guideline:

Dear heavenly Father,

I acknowledge I have sinned and cannot pay the price to put things right. I am sorry.

Thank you for sending Jesus Christ to take the penalty for my sin.

Thank you that Jesus Christ died on the cross and you raised him to life so that I may now have a relationship with you. I accept, by faith, all that Jesus Christ did on my behalf.

I confess that Jesus is Lord and Saviour of my life from this moment forward.

Thank you for saving me! In Jesus' name I pray. Amen.

It is great that you have decided to become a Christian and followed through by asking Jesus into your life. I would encourage you to tell someone you trust about your decision and find a local Bible-believing church you can be a part of.

APPENDIX 2

Bible Version

All Bible verses are from the New International Version (NIV) except where specified.

CEB – Common English Bible

CEV – Contemporary English Version

CSB – Christian Standard Bible

ESV – English Standard Version

GNT – Good News Translation

GW - God's Word Translation

HCSB - Holman Christian Standard Bible

ISV - International Standard Version

KJV - King James Version

KJV 2000 - King James 2000 Bible

MSG – The Message

NASB - New American Standard Bible

NET - New English Translation

NKJV - New King James Version

NLT - New Living Translation

PHILLIPS - J.B. Phillips New Testament

RSV - Revised Standard Version

TLB – Living Bible

APPENDIX 3

References:

Page 19 - Proverbs 3:12

Page 65 - Psalm 68:19

Page 85 - 1 Chronicles 29:11

Page 87 - 1 Corinthians 13:4-8 (TLB)

Page 105 - Ephesians 2:6

Page 107 - Colossians 3:3 (MSG)

Page 127 - John 8:12

Page 129 - Matthew 5:44

Page 139 - Judges 6:12 - 16

Page 155 - Isaiah 41:10

Page 167 - Isaiah 55:11

Page 183 - Psalm 127:2

Page 201 - John 14:9

Page 203 - Jeremiah 24:6 & Romans 8:32 (PHILLIPS)

Lightning Source UK Ltd.
Milton Keynes UK
UKHW011833021118
331659UK00003B/91/P